I0733696

LINDA SAMMARITAN

DANCING
IN THE
SILENCE

By Linda Sammaritan

This book is dedicated to my mother,
Barbara E. Geib.

She is one of those military spouses who
soldiered on alone while her soulmate
deployed to war. Her strength and courage in
raising four children, one of them with special
needs, are an inspiration to me.

May I live with the same determination
to gain victory over uncertain times.

The Lord has given me the passion to write.
With gratitude and praise, I offer this gift to Him.

Acknowledgments

Dancing in the Silence is a work of fiction, but many of the episodes are true.

When I look back on that rough eighteen months of my childhood, there are so many people who made our lives better with their support. Over fifty years later, I can't remember all the names, but I do remember that members of St. Mark's Episcopal Church, friends in town, and old friends from across the country closed ranks to protect us. A special thank you to Laurie, who was the best friend an unconfident girl could have in the midst of eighth-grade emotions and whose father was at war. Also, I'd like to honor the memory of Mrs. Bellringer, my choir director, who helped me build back some self-confidence from my deep well of self-pity. I know she did the same for many other students.

The same critique groups who helped me perfect *Reaching Into Silence* were my best teachers for this sequel as well. Lady Lits, Heartland Writers, Indianapolis Writers Meet-Up, and Scriblerians. And in these last few days of polish, you were invaluable!

Tim, thank you for harping on me to add details. When I objected that the book would be too long for a young adult novel, you were the one who said, "Then make it more than one book." And voilá! The entire series almost wrote itself from that point on.

Cynthia, Beth, and Steve, you have been my personal copy editors and proofreaders. Without you, this book would still be suffering from too many commas, awkward sentences, and a story arc full of holes.

Joyce and John, you have helped me see the big picture within each chapter.

Thank you, Cynthia Hickey and Winged Publications, for your patience as I learn the ropes of publishing. You are wonderfully efficient in answering all of my questions

My husband, my family, and my friends have cheered me on as they see this series become the printed page. What would I do without all of you? And I love it when you ask me, "When is the next book coming out?"

Well, here it is.

A Note to the Deaf Community

The World Without Sound series begins in 1965 and ends in 1970. At that time, the medical and educational establishments were convinced sign language did more harm than good, believing deaf children would never learn to communicate with the hearing world.

These were years where the schools demanded "speech only" education. Hearing parents, deaf children, and many teachers ended up feeling even more defeated in an already-frustrating situation. It wasn't until later in the Seventies that ASL was considered an acceptable alternative, and my sister's school taught both sign language and speech. I believe the combination was labeled "total communication," although today, that term includes cued speech, SEE, and other sign languages.

While I have noticed some contention on both trains of thought to this day, I believe ASL is more accepted as a viable means of communication than it was fifty years ago, and our deaf children grow up with far less stress.

A Note to the 21st Century Reader

Language evolves with each generation. What was an acceptable word or phrase in another century or even five years ago, may be condemned as derogatory or hateful today.

To be true to the era of the 1960s, you may find some of my terminology offensive, particularly the label of "mentally retarded." However, the term was acceptable to both medical and educational professionals. In fact, my first state teaching license contained these words as my specialty: "Mildly Mentally Retarded."

In the World Without Sound series, I considered changing the term to "cognitively challenged" or "developmentally disabled," but modern phrases throw the reader into present times instead of what the world was really like fifty years ago and more.

Within the narrative, I have tried to make sure the reader understands which words were medically appropriate and which were intended as insults. And believe me, main character Debbie more than bristles at the cruelty she occasionally meets in others!

Chapter 1:
The Best Thing and the Worst Thing (February 1967)

Last summer, Fwan-nee
Saved me from dogs in a barn.
I like Fwan-nee now.

Leaf shadows danced in the sliver of a moonbeam reflected on the bedroom wall. I yawned and snuggled under the covers while Francie fussed with her pillow on the other side of the room. The best thing in the world was this moment, getting to visit my oldest friend for three whole days.

"Debbie?"

"Mm-hmm."

The heat ticking through the baseboards created a cozy lullaby.

"We haven't talked about the *worst* thing." Francie and I used to have sleepovers every Friday night when I lived around the block, and we always talked about the best thing and the worst thing of the week.

I'd spent the last month *ignoring* the worst thing in my life.

"Now or later?" Her voice died to a whisper.

"Now. Then we can get up tomorrow and have fun."

Like killing mold by exposing it to sunlight, we needed to toss out all of our sadness where we could see it clearly instead of letting it lurk in dim corners. Then *maybe* we could enjoy the rest of my stay.

Francie turned on the bedside lamp, creating a soft glow from the milk glass. "I'll start."

Even after she'd crushed her honey-brown hair on the pillow, it draped silky and smooth over one shoulder. My frizzy blond waves never looked that good.

Francie's deep blue eyes glittered with tears. "My dad has a new job, and we're moving to Idaho."

Back in January, she'd told me the news over the phone. It was bad enough when I moved to the opposite end of New York State after fifth grade. Now, we'd live even farther apart. Who could take time for a road trip across the country? And nobody was rich enough to fly. We might not ever see each other again.

I stared at the Beatles poster on the wall above the dresser. John Lennon, who always seemed to brood over the problems in life, peered back at me. My old Tressy doll sat on top of the dresser. Her perky smile created an odd contrast with his solemn expression. "What's the worst thing about moving?"

Francie's tears spilled over. "I'll never see Ernie again."

I'd feel the same way if my boyfriend, Chip, were gone from my life forever. "Are you going to write to each other?”

"Probably. But I haven't told him yet. What if he breaks up with me *now* so it won't hurt so bad later?”

"If he's that much of a weenie, he's not good enough for you.”

She hiccupped a laugh through her tears and sniffed. "Thanks.”

"What's the best thing about moving?”

Paul McCartney's face smiled at me from the poster. His upbeat personality kicked aside John's glum attitude.

She thought for a moment. "I'll get to ski in the Rocky Mountains. They'll make the Adirondacks feel like bunny hills.”

"Then I'd better not visit you in winter.”

Francie snorted. She knew I was terrified of skiing. "We'd have to be on the lookout for bears in the summer.”

"Better than swimming with sharks, right?” *She* was terrified of the ocean.

Our giggles brought a parental voice from the other side of the wall. "Girls.”

Francie turned off the lamp. Your turn,” she whispered. "Worst thing.”

All of my laughter drained away. "We're moving to California next month so my dad can train for Vietnam.” The idea of my father being in danger every day for a whole year hovered over me like a dark parachute descending to the ground and burying me underneath folds of fear.

In the moonlight, her eyes widened. "Will he have to bomb villages?”

"I don't know. I think he's supposed to shoot

enemy planes."

We never talked about these things at home. I couldn't picture my father killing anybody. He was the nicest, kindest dad in the world, but...he was a fighter pilot.

"Have you seen all the protests on the news?" Francie was full of uncomfortable questions.

"We try not to watch." What if she was like the people on TV, screaming and swearing at any man in a uniform? Would she hate me because my dad was in the Air Force? "What do *you* think of the war protests?"

She shook her head. "I don't know. Those people are so nasty. But I guess I do wonder why we're in a war at all."

How had Daddy explained it?

"Before we were born, communists in North Korea tried to take over South Korea, and we went to war to stop them. Now, communists in North Vietnam are trying to take over South Vietnam, and we have to do it again."

"Why not just let them be communist?"

"Because the people in the south don't want to be, and we're their friends. If we don't help our friends, they'll lose the war, and then the communists will try to take over Cambodia and Burma and Laos and Thailand."

"And those people don't want to be communist either, I guess." Silence for a few seconds while she paused to consider strangers halfway around the world. "What's the worst thing about moving to California?"

"My dad could die."

If I didn't want to watch the news, and I didn't want to think about what my dad might have to do in a war, I sure didn't want to think about him dying. I'd never even said those words out loud before. To stop her from asking any more questions, I rushed on with my list of "next-worsts."

"Then there's other stuff, like I won't see Chip for months. I'll have to make new friends and then leave almost as soon as I've gotten to know them. Without Dad around to referee, my mother will drive me crazy. But I'm the oldest kid, so I'll be expected to help out, especially with Krista. What if I mess up?" I paused for breath. "And I'll be living in a desert with rattlesnakes, scorpions, black widows, and who knows what else that can kill a person."

I didn't appreciate Francie's snicker.

"If it were that dangerous, *nobody* would survive in California. There's an awful lot of people there."

"Maybe, but I'll be praying for angels to protect me every night while I sleep."

"You do that." The smile remained in her voice. "What's the best thing?"

Easy answer. "After four months, I get to go back home to Hampton Shores and the ocean."

"That doesn't count. What's the best thing in *California?*"

Chapter Two:
Goodbye, Francie

Fwan-nee's house is cold.
There is lots of snow outside.
I can slide in snow.

It took me a second, but I came up with one good thing about the desert. "Now that we know for sure my little sister is deaf, she doesn't have to see any doctors while we're there."

Francie settled onto her side. "So, how did you find out Krista's deaf? I remember when we visited last summer you were teaching her sign language. I thought you were crazy."

"Because the *doctors* said she was mentally retarded, and she'd never learn anything?"

Francie's face pinked up, visible in the moonlight. She'd always blushed easily. "Well…doctors are usually the experts."

I had been so mad at those doctors.

She persisted. "So, what changed their minds?"

"You remember that awful hospital I wrote you about? Where Krista had the operation to sew up the hole in her heart the year before?"

Gray. The place was so gray. Gray linoleum, gray walls. Even infant Krista had looked gray.

Francie's voice softened in the darkness. "Yeah, I thought she was going to die there. I felt really bad for you."

I had felt bad for me, too. "She went back there for two weeks after Christmas while they poked her with needles and tested her for all sorts of things. They even did a spinal tap, put a big needle right between the bones in her back."

Francie sucked in her breath. "Owww. And she's so little."

"It gave her a horrible headache." Even Daddy was upset the day of the spinal tap. I swallowed back guilty tears. "I wouldn't even visit her, and I was finally old enough."

"I don't blame you. If Vinnie was hurting that bad, I couldn't stand seeing it."

"If I'd gone there, I would've wanted to snatch her out of bed and run as far away as I could."

Francie chuckled. "I can see you sneaking through the halls, making a break for the front door, and—then what? Hide out in the middle of New York City?"

"That's why I didn't visit her. There was nothing I could do. But I feel like I let her down anyway."

The sheets rustled as Francie sat up, hair haloed by the moonlight. "What if you had?"

"What?"

"Kidnapped her, got to the city, and hid in one of those huge department stores? The two of you hand in hand, browsing through the latest fashions. There are restrooms. And coffee shops. You would have had it all! Food, clothes, a roof over your head! And *no doctors.*"

Francie still knew how to cheer me up.

She settled back into bed. "So, obviously, they found out she's deaf. Anything else?"

"That's the biggest thing, I guess. And now that we know she has to see what we say, we're really careful that we're looking right at her when we talk to her. She already knows a few more words just by reading our lips" I grinned. "It's my new mission in life—I'm going to teach her to talk. But I'm still teaching her sign language."

"What words does she say?"

"She doesn't *say* anything. Yet." I heaved a sigh. "But she understands some words that *we* say, like *Mom*, of course, and *Debbie, Paul, Wade. Milk.*" I grinned. "And *Boo-boo.* Except she gets it mixed up with *poo-poo.*"

That always brought a snicker from people. Francie was no exception.

"The other big thing is she's got cerebral palsy in her legs, which is why she was late in walking."

"I saw she wobbles around on tiptoe, sort of."

"She can't stand with her feet flat on the floor. Her muscles are too tight. So, she's going to get leg braces once we're back home."

Francie turned on the lamp again, and I pulled the blankets over my eyes to avoid the blinding light. When I peeked out, she'd opened a drawer in the little table between our beds and plucked out a stubby pencil and a little memo pad.

"You're gonna make a list now? It's after midnight." I stifled another yawn. Francie and her lists.

Some things never change.

She talked while she wrote. "Number One, hole in heart. Number Two, deaf. Number three, cerebral palsy." She looked my way, pencil poised in mid-air. "What else did they find out?"

"She's blind in the eye that was clouded by the cataract." I rolled onto my side as she wrote Number Four. "She'll have an operation for that, too, but she still won't be able to see things. Only light and shadows."

"Whoa. Deaf *and* partly blind." With raised eyebrows, Francie scribbled more notes, then looked up. "Anything else?"

The bland question pushed my hot button. "How much else do you want there to be?"

"I didn't mean…I was just…I was trying to think how each problem could be fixed. I didn't *want* more problems."

It wasn't Francie's fault that she didn't live with leg-stretching exercises and daily tantrums. "Yeah. I've done the same thing, trying to figure out a fix."

Francie hopped out of bed and squeezed me in a hug before I finished my sentence. All was forgiven.

As we sat side by side on my bed, I instructed her to add one more item to the list. "Number Five, high IQ."

She obediently wrote it down. "How did they know?"

I grinned. "Probably during the best part of her days at the hospital. They watched her play."

"They can tell something like that from watching kids play?"

"I guess. They said she has her own imaginary

games, and when they taught her how to use a new toy, she got it right away."

"They had to put her in a hospital to figure that out?" She shook her head as the drawer squeaked open and she put away the pencil and paper.

"I *know*. I kept saying she was smart and could do all kinds of stuff, but doctors wouldn't listen to a kid. They wouldn't listen to my parents either."

Francie returned to the practical. "So, they fixed her heart, she'll get braces, nothing will help her eye, and she can hear with the hearing aids."

"I don't know how much she can hear with them. When Mom first puts them in, Krista screeches and has a fit. She hates them."

"Do they hurt?"

"I don't think so. I think she hears something, but there also seems to be a lot of scratchy sounds like when you can't get a radio station to come in clearly. She doesn't like it. And sometimes, they make a squealing noise, and it hurts *my* ears. Maybe it hurts hers, too, when they do that."

There was nothing more to say. We stared at each other in silence.

"Oh, I almost forgot to show you." Francie retrieved Tressy from the dresser. The doll's hair had been combed into an updo with corkscrew curls perfectly arranged to frame her face. "I threw out my Barbie dolls and the baby dolls, but this one's special."

Francie handed her over. A folded piece of paper was still tucked between her neck and the front of her dress. I couldn't believe it. "You kept the note, too?" When we moved to Hampton Shores, I left Tressy behind along with a message written as if the doll had penned it.

"You want to take it out and read it?" Francie offered me a smile so bright that light flashed off her braces.

With two fingers, I gingerly tugged out the note. Red crayon spelled the word "FRANCIE." The paper crackled a little as I unfolded it and smoothed it out, a message from one sad little fifth-grade girl to another. "Debbie says I can stay." A heart split with a zigzag break covered the bottom corner.

More words, in pencil, followed in Francie's careful, cursive handwriting. "Debbie will be my best friend forever."

I brushed a tear from my cheek before looking up. A matching tear rolled down Francie's face. Even if we never saw each other again, the words on the note would stay true.

We talked for hours. About old friends and new friends and boyfriends. About junior high and changing classes and which clubs we had joined. About church and ice skating with the youth group come Sunday night. About The Beatles versus The Monkees—who was better? We talked until a pink hint of sunrise peeked through the window, and we drifted into slumber.

Best friends forever.

Chapter 3:
The Day Before Moving Day

More and more boxes.
I have fun climbing on them.
Mah-mi should keep them.

My last day of school.

If only I could cut this day out of my life the way movie producers cut and splice film. But then I would lose the bittersweet memories of goodbyes.

If only this day would last forever so I wouldn't have to move. No, that wouldn't work either. I'd never get to see Daddy again. He'd left for California a month ago.

I was stuck with a normal day for everybody else except me. Life wouldn't be normal until Daddy came back from Vietnam, more than a year away.

When the bell rang signaling the end of music class, Mr. Basso asked me to stay. "We're going to miss you, especially in the soprano section."

I ducked my head and studied the black squiggles on the blue floor tiles.

Bending down to face me, his long bangs fell across his eyes. "Are you going to sign up for the choir in your new school?" He attempted a grin. "You'd better." But he sobered when I wouldn't respond. I pressed my lips tight, trying not to cry.

Straightening up, he patted my shoulder, that tentative kind, fingertips only, when a person doesn't know what to do. "I imagine this is pretty difficult, moving in the middle of the school year."

I nodded but still couldn't speak for fear of losing it.

"I'm disappointed, too." He sighed.

Why would he be disappointed? *He* got to stay here and enjoy his job and keep his home and live with his wife, while I had to leave, move into a strange house, and say goodbye to my dad this summer.

Last fall, I'd planned to try out for the lead in the junior high spring musical. I would've gotten it. I was *good*. That dream, like so many others for seventh grade, crumbled to dust. Melissa would be the star instead. Meanwhile, Mr. Basso made me sing with the chorus once rehearsals started, even though I wouldn't be there for the performance.

He took one last stab at offering encouragement as he handed me a late pass and sent me on to my next class. "I'm sure you'll be given a solo in your next school."

Maybe. So what?

The next hurdle was saying goodbye to all my friends after school let out. If I thought driving away from Francie's house was a killer last month, this felt worse. But at least I'd be back with my Hampton Shores friends before the summer ended.

Melissa draped her tall, slender, highly-perfumed self over my head and shoulders. "I'll miss you so much! I'll write. You write to me, too. You've got my address, right?"

I couldn't answer with my face smushed against her arm.

After she peeled herself off of me, Leigh took her place. She squeezed me so hard I couldn't breathe. Her tears soaked through my sweater. "I can't believe you're leaving. This can't be happening. I'll write. Every week. I'll keep you posted on everything that's going on. I'll even go to all the track meets and let you know how Chip does."

"Thanks," I managed to breathe out.

A lot of the guys made sure to give me a hug, too. The buses rolled out. Finally, Chip and I were left alone outside the front doors.

He didn't say anything.

Watching his lips turn blue as we shivered in the icy wind, I said, "I'll miss you so much." *Obviously.* Dumb, Debbie. Dumb. Dumb. Dumb.

"Me, too."

That was it. We stood there and waited for the "late" buses, the ones that take kids home after sports practices, music rehearsals, and club meetings. My bus arrived, its engine hissing to a stop. Stinky, black smoke puffed from its back end. As soon as the doors folded open, several kids hurried onto it, eager to get out of the cold.

I looked at Chip. Would he kiss me goodbye? We still had never done anything more romantic than hold hands. I blinked back tears. "I guess I'll see you before school starts next year. I'll write."

He nodded, then bent forward. I closed my eyes, and he brushed his lips…on my cheek. "Bye, Debbie."

I climbed the two steps, found a seat, and gazed out the window. Chip remained where I'd left him, his coat collar pulled up around his ears. He waved as the bus pulled away. With no one seated close to me, I let the tears fall. Not only because I would miss Chip, but disappointment whispered through me. What had I expected? That he'd sweep me into his arms and carry me away like Rhett Butler did with Scarlet O'Hara in *Gone with the Wind?*

One last thing.

Mom drove me to Cathy Morris's house. We knew each other from church, but Cathy was a year behind me in school. The moms had "made arrangements" for my two goldfish, the only pets that had ever survived in our family for more than a year.

George and Marty swam in small circles in the fishbowl resting on my lap. They were so old their orange scales had faded to a peach-tinted silver. Mom refused to ship them special to California, and there was no way I could take them on the plane. If we had a dog, we would have taken *him.*

Cathy answered my knock and took the bag of fish food and supplies. She led me down a narrow hall to her bedroom where she'd cleared a space on top of a bookshelf. "You can set the bowl here." She plopped the bag next to it.

"I left directions on the bag, so you know how much food to give them and how often."

"Okay."

We watched George and Marty dart from one side of the bowl to the opposite side. They knew something was up.

"I had to take some of their water out so it wouldn't spill on the way over. Can we get a pitcher and fill their bowl?"

"Okay."

We trotted back to the kitchen. Mrs. Morris handed the pitcher to Cathy who handed it to me. I filled it at the sink.

"Y'all look so solemn." Mrs. Morris squeezed my shoulder. "We'll take good care of your fish. What are their names?"

"George and Marty."

"Got that, Cathy?"

"Yup." Cathy nodded her head vigorously.

Back in the bedroom, I poured the water, trying to aim between the two fish. Usually, I scooped them out with a net and placed them in a small bowl of water while I cleaned their home. The stream from the pitcher must have been startling, maybe even terrifying.

"I also put in directions on how to clean their bowl. Do it about once a week."

"Okay."

I handed her the empty pitcher. "Don't you even want to look at the directions?"

She shrugged. "I can do it later. You just sprinkle in the food, right?"

"Pretty much. Cleaning is a little trickier."

"My mom will help the first couple of times." She headed out of the room, letting the pitcher dangle from one finger.

I stroked the glass bowl as if I could pet George and Marty. "Bye, little guys. I'll see you in a few months."

Could they make it without me until July? I wasn't sure if *I* could survive that long.

Chapter 4:
Moving Out

Mah-mi walks back and
Forth. The boys fight. In-nee's here!
So, nothing is wrong.

I shoved a spoonful of soggy bran flakes into my mouth while Krista let the same stuff dribble out of hers. The movers would be here in an hour, and it was snowing like crazy.

Mom paced the kitchen, stopped to stare out the window, and strode back to the table. "I can't believe we have to move out in the middle of a blizzard."

She exaggerated under stress. If this were a real blizzard, the movers would've postponed their arrival. No. This was a run-of-the-mill snowstorm with six to ten inches expected by the end of the day.

We could've gotten out of school, but it was Saturday. We could've spent our day in and out of the house building snow forts and snowmen, making snow angels, or sledding down the hill a block from our house. But our snow clothes were packed for storage.

Nope. The boys and I could either help with the move and the cleaning or stay out of the way. With absolutely nothing else to do, we'd be helping. The *whole* day.

Wade pulled some stupid plastic car out of the cereal box, and Paul grabbed it from him.

"Hey, I found it first." Wade tried to grab it back while Paul lifted it high above his head.

Too short to reach the prize, Wade belted Paul in the stomach. Paul still didn't let go, but with his free hand, he shoved Wade back into his seat. Milk sloshed from his bowl, onto the table, and dripped off the edge.

Mom slapped a dish rag in Wade's hand and plucked the car out of Paul's. "Boys, cut it out. I don't need this today."

"But I had it first."

Mom gave Wade her tight-lipped, squinty-eyed, evil-mother look. "Whoever remembers it first at the end of the day can have it." She turned the same expression on Paul. "And if it ends up a race, it goes in the garbage."

As soon as Wade mopped up the spill, she took the clammy, milk-soaked dish rag and handed it to me. "When Krista is done, wash all the bowls and silverware, and put them in the open box on the counter. Stick the dish soap in there, too."

There were three kids capable of washing dishes here, but I was the lucky winner. Could this day end up any worse than yesterday?

Mom returned to pacing. "I can*not* believe we have to move out in the middle of a blizzard." Back and forth, back and forth, from the kitchen door to the hallway. She reminded me of a caged tiger.

"*I* can't believe you won't let me take my tent," Paul said. He'd been whining about that for two days, ever since he realized his precious Boy Scout pup tent was on the list of items to be stored.

"Don't start with me about that." Mom spun around, a finger pointed sharply at him.

"Can we at least buy one while we're out there?" he pleaded. "I want to camp in the desert."

"Absolutely not. You'll wake up with scorpions all over you."

Paul slouched in his chair, chin almost resting on the table. "When we come home, it better not be full of moth holes."

An old brown sedan rolled into our driveway. Mrs. Richards, Mom's friend from church. She left the car running and scurried toward the door to our garage, the shortest route to the house.

Mom hurried to Krista, wiped her milk-and-cereal-glopped face with the bib, and snatched her out of the highchair. Without knocking, Mrs. Richards entered the kitchen, a blast of frosty air her companion.

Mom tugged Krista's hat over her head and tied the strings under her chin. "Thanks so much for doing this, Jenny." She jammed Krista's arm into the sleeve of her coat while forcing a smile on her own face. "You got here early. I thought the snow would certainly cause a delay."

"I wanted to get going before it got any worse out there." Mrs. Richards smiled at Krista and held out her arms. "Are you ready to come to my house and play with the baby?"

Krista grinned and strained against Mom's efforts at buttoning her coat.

That's what I loved about Mrs. Richards. Not only was she beautiful with doe-brown eyes that reminded me of the glamorous actress Sophia Loren, she talked to Krista as if everything were normal. She knew Krista couldn't hear her words, but the lady was so expressive with her face and hands, Krista seemed to know what she was saying.

She staggered on her toes, mittened hands outstretched, toward Mrs. Richards. Mom had decided no leg braces for the day. Krista would have to wear them for such a long time tomorrow.

Paul grumbled over his cereal bowl. "At least *some*one's going to have fun today."

Mrs. Richards's head swiveled from Paul to Mom. "Why didn't you tell me the others had no place to play? If they can hurry and get ready, I'll take them all home with me."

Paul lifted his chin to get Mom in his sights. Did we have a chance?

"They can't go outside in this mess to play. Everything's packed." Mom sounded apologetic.

Mrs. Richards waved a hand in dismissal. "Frankie and Paul are the same size. We have spare clothes, and I'm sure I can find some of Frankie's old stuff for Wade." She examined me with the practiced eye of a seamstress. "Debbie's gotten so tall, she'll probably fit in something of mine."

Actually, I was taller than Mrs. Richards.

All three of us waited for Mom's verdict.

"Well…" Mom's tone of surrender. "The boys can go with you." Their whoops and the scraping of chairs pushed away from the table interrupted her sentence. "But I really need help once the movers get here." She turned to me with a sympathetic smile. "I'm sorry, Debbie. You're going to have to stay."

My day just got worse. Like Sara Crewe in *A Little Princess*, I was forced into slavery to Miss Minchin, alias Mom.

After I washed dishes, I spent the next hour checking each of the boxes which had been packed by the moving company. Was the box labeled with its contents and the room it belonged in? Check. Was it taped securely? Check. Was there an identifying sticker from the moving company attached? Check.

As the huge van pulled up to the house, Mom Minchin provided me with final instructions. "Once a room is clear of furniture and boxes, dust mop the floor, make sure the closets are empty, wash the windows, and dust any other woodwork. Everything you need is in the bathroom."

Gee, what was left for her to do? Once again, she read my mind. "I'll have the master inventory list and check each item as it leaves the house."

We watched two burly men wearing heavy-duty boots and bulky jackets tromp through the snow-covered yard to our front door. She sighed. "And somehow, I'm supposed to keep this house move-in ready for the next occupants."

A rap on the door. Mom opened it. The men stepped in, snow immediately melting off their boots. "Mizz Hansen? Y'all ready?"

Mom's slight smile didn't reach her eyes. "As ready as we're going to be."

"We're gonna do a walk-through and see how we want to proceed in fillin' the truck."

Mom stepped aside, and the men made wet tracks

on the wood floors all the way to the back bedrooms. I heard them mumbling to each other, catching words like "mattress" and "dressers." On their return, they halted in the living room where most of the heavy furniture sat. "We better start with the piano, then the sofa, then take apart the hutch."

I cringed at the thought of my piano going out into snow and then to a warehouse. Mom would have to get it tuned once we were in our new home in town this summer. Could storage kill a piano?

At least the morning went by more pleasantly than I expected. Not one room was empty of furniture and boxes until after lunch. The men thumped and bumped—and occasionally crashed—with all of our heavy items, while I sat in my closet with the door open to let in light and read from my hidden stash of books. Just like the Little Princess in her attic garret.

A little after five o'clock, we stared at the wreck of an empty house. The scent of lemon oil emanated from every windowsill. Unfortunately, it mixed with a mustiness from the dirty snow puddles the movers left behind in the front entryway. Mom leaned against a bare wall, staring blankly at the wet floor. A blister on the inside of my thumb proved my dust-mopping skills.

As much as I wanted to grab my coat out of the closet, we weren't done yet, even though we'd promised Mrs. Richards we'd be at her place for supper. And with only a peanut butter and jelly sandwich for lunch, a stale one that had been made yesterday, I was looking forward to a good dinner.

Mom shook her head and pushed off from the wall. "The housing inspector is not going to be happy." Her fingertips massaged her temples. "But there's nothing more to be done. No mop, no bucket, no towels."

"Want me to run next door and ask for some?" The last thing I wanted to do was make my way through eight inches of snow without boots, but Sara Crewe would have.

"Thanks, sweetie, but no. I can't stand the thought of handing them back a pile of filthy, soggy towels." She offered me a tired smile. "Do we have any paper towels left?"

I ran to the bathroom and returned with less than half a roll. She tore off a dozen squares and handed me the rest.

"Let's sop up what we can with this, and then we'll leave."

Those puddles must have been just over the freezing point. My hands felt like ice by the time I used all my paper towels and the dried-out dish rag from the morning. A thin sheen of dampness still covered the floor, but it would dry within the hour.

Mom crammed the cardboard tube into the already stuffed trash box. "Put this last one in the garage, turn the lock as you leave, and wait for me. I'll take the keys next door."

The neighbors would meet the housing inspector on Monday, when we'd be thirty thousand feet over Kansas.

I zipped up my coat, then casually, and with great satisfaction, I slid the stupid plastic car off the counter and into the trash. A slight rustling and gentle thump told me it had reached the bottom. Before I gave into the temptation to wander through the empty rooms and get sentimental, I dragged the garbage out the door and locked up.

Mom returned, started the car, and I stayed to the side ready to pull down the garage door and secure it. As soon as the back tires reached deep snow, they started to spin. She gunned it in reverse all the way to the road. My horrible day would be even worse if we got stuck in the driveway that used to be ours until five minutes ago.

The door came down with a rumble, and I used a tire track to run to the car, which Mom had maneuvered so the passenger door was in my direct path. After kicking snow off my shoes, I slammed shut the door, and we rolled down the street, snowflakes dancing in our headlights, no sound but the hum of the engine.

Mom never looked back, but I did. This was the house where Krista was born, where we waited for news if she would live or die. This was where she came home from open-heart surgery, where she got healthy again. This was where I started a summer nursery school for neighborhood kids, and where Krista learned to walk.

No tears though. Maybe I used them all after yesterday's afternoon bus ride. The outline of my home faded as the car gained speed on the plowed street. Goodbye, Stuart Rd. Goodbye, Suffolk Air Force Base. I loved you.

Chapter 5:
Welcome to the Desert California

The plane goes up, up.
When it goes down, we will see
Da-di. I've missed him.

aul thought I was being extra nice to let him and Wade trade off on the window seats for both flights. Ha. I kept the aisle seat so I could be the first one off the plane. Nobody, not my brothers, not Mom, would prevent me from being the first to see Daddy.

As soon as we taxied to a stop at Los Angeles International Airport, I hopped up and grabbed my assigned bag from the overhead compartment. I didn't even wait for the announcement that we could unfasten our seat belts.

Wade used the palm of his hand to push on my stomach and move me backwards. "Let me out."

I used my whole body to push back. "It's too crowded. You'll get your turn once the line starts moving."

When the lady in front of me shuffled forward, he

tried it again, but I shoved past him and pressed against the lady's giant pocketbook hanging by its strap off her shoulder. People behind us let my brothers into the aisle. I don't know how he did it from the window seat, but somehow Paul leaped ahead of Wade, and then he tried to wiggle between me and the seats while the planeload of passengers was still squeezed together like a closed accordion. Once we were on the corridor ramp to the terminal, I swung the bag into Paul's knees every time he tried to walk ahead of me.

As we stepped into the passenger waiting area, I scanned the crowd for Daddy. There! My heart and feet zoomed into overdrive. I almost ran over the pocketbook lady as I barreled into him for a hug. The boys squashed me from behind, and the scent of pipe tobacco mixed with Daddy's deodorant sent me to a safe place. For the first time in weeks, I was happy. Maybe California wouldn't be so bad.

Daddy's crew cut had been bleached from the sun, and he was tan. He planted a kiss on top of each of our heads. "You three have grown so much in a month, if you all attack me like this in a year, I'll be flat on the floor."

We giggled, then stared at him, all three of us tongue-tied.

Daddy looked over our heads. "Where's your mother and Krista?"

Wasn't she right behind us? Passenger after passenger stepped from the corridor into the waiting area, but no Mom.

Wade patted Daddy's arm as if to reassure him. "She was in the next row. We didn't fly here by ourselves."

With a chuckle, Daddy tousled Wade's hair.

After the last passenger straggled through the gate with two bags under each arm, Mom strolled out. She held Krista in her arms and chatted with a stewardess, who carried the diaper bag, Mom's purse, and an extra duffle bag. After all the tension of getting to the airport on time, then rushing for our connecting flight, Mom looked like she'd just spent the day relaxing on the beach with her friends.

When she reached the rest of us, she shifted Krista to one hip and hugged the stewardess. "Thanks for all your help. Enjoy your week off."

The stewardess smiled. "I will. Welcome to California." With a nod to Daddy, she disappeared into the crowd.

Mom leaned into Daddy for a kiss. Krista, who'd had all her attention on the retreating stewardess, shrieked when she noticed Daddy. Almost leaping out of Mom's arms, she clung to him, covering his face with kisses before snuggling against his shoulder.

Mom handed Wade the duffle bag. "I believe this is yours."

He hung his head. "I forgot. Sorry."

Daddy, with one arm supporting Krista and the other wrapped around Mom's shoulders, herded us into the river of passengers heading for baggage claim.

We'd left our big boat of a station wagon with civilian friends until we returned to New York, so for now, we'd make do with one little, and I mean *little,* blue Renault for the months in between. It had about as much space as a Volkswagen Beetle. Maybe less.

Daddy stuffed the larger suitcases into the trunk. Then we squeezed into the narrow seats with the leftover carry-on items. We wedged shoe bags, toy bags, and duffel bags between our bodies, under our feet, and on our laps. I could finally understand why we carried Krista all over three airports. Nowhere to stow a stroller.

"We only have to endure this sardine can for two hours," Daddy assured us.

A sardine can that had been sitting in an oven. We'd started this trip bundled in our coats. Those got left behind with Mr. Fadler once he dropped us off at LaGuardia Airport. Good thing. We would have died of heat exhaustion before ever reaching our new home.

Wade wiped the sweat off his face with my cotton jacket. I didn't complain. A small price to pay for having Daddy back. Besides, I'd only needed the extra layer on the air-conditioned plane anyway.

Daddy slammed the trunk and slid into the driver's seat. He was the only one with any space. "Got to be able to use the brake and the clutch without getting tangled in *stuff*." He turned back to us kids before switching on the ignition. "Got enough room back there?" And he laughed, which made me and Paul and Wade laugh, too.

Mom, loaded down with Krista on her lap and surrounded by the diaper bag, her purse, and our snack bag, pointed a finger at him. "Ha. Ha."

And away we went.

Paul stuck his head out the window. "Whoa! Those mountains look like a pile of rocks."

"You'll get to see them up close and personal."

Daddy reached back and tapped the duffel bag on Paul's lap. "You want your head chopped off?"

Paul ducked back in on the double.

As we approached San Bernardino, Mom passed back a bottle of water for the three of us to share. Paul dribbled a portion over his neck. Wade copied him. I drank my third, then ran my cool tongue over my dry lips.

The gravel-looking rocks had grown to huge boulders towering over the car.

"Do they ever have rockslides around here?" I asked. "We'd be flattened like a tin can under an eighteen-wheeler."

"Sometimes, but they haven't had any earthquakes lately to shake them loose."

Add earthquakes to my list of dangers to survive in this foreign country, but being a flatlander, I didn't get bored with the view. Wild mountains, giant boulders, and sand stretching as far as I could see. Francie was right. Even the Adirondack Mountains in upstate New York were green hills compared to the stony crags towering over us.

We took a break from our tight quarters halfway through the drive and stopped at a diner for a meal. It seemed to be an old railroad car, all metal and painted with blue horizontal stripes, kind of like something on the set of *Route 66.*

I slithered out from between the bags as a blast of desert heat and the intoxicating aroma of grilled burgers welcomed me. With my short skirt, I made sure my hind end was toward the car, not the road, as I stretched cramped legs by bending over and touching my toes. Straightening up, I noticed people in the restaurant laughing. I turned to where they pointed.

Us?

We looked like a clown act at the circus. One tiny car with more and more people climbing out of it. Paul popped out on the driver's side. Wade tumbled through the door I'd exited, followed by a shoe bag he knocked off the seat. Mom shimmied out as she juggled her purse, the diaper bag, and Krista. Daddy opened the trunk, and all anyone could see of him was his backside as he rearranged the suitcases.

"Debbie," Mom called. "Please take Krista off my hands while I reorganize in here." Without waiting for my response, she set a sleepy Krista on her feet. What a little trooper. She hadn't once complained. Not about getting up at dawn, not about the plane ride, not about this heat.

I grabbed Krista's hand before she fell. Since getting leg braces, the poor baby had to learn to walk all over again, and she was still wobbly. Without my asking, Paul took Krista's other hand. His eyes met mine, and we nodded to each other. If the audience on the other side of the windows found Krista's braces to be part of our comedy act, we'd hold our heads high. We were family, and that's what mattered.

By the time we finished our meal, nobody paid attention to the tiny girl in braces or the family that repacked itself into the little blue car. Stale sweat hung in the air, and we immediately opened every window all the way. With an average speed of fifteen to twenty miles an hour, the rest of the trip took another two hours as we chugged up the mountain, higher and higher.

"I'm sorry, Dorothy." Daddy massaged the back of

Mom's neck. Krista nestled against her, sound asleep. "I didn't take into account that it was two hours *down*hill to the airport. Traveling uphill is more of a strain. This poor, overloaded, little transmission has to growl down into first or second gear every time we take a steep turn."

And there were plenty of hairpin turns up the mountain before we pulled into the driveway of our new home.

The air had cooled with the disappearance of the sun. Jacket-less, I hurried from the car into the house. Daddy had told us all about it. Bigger than it looked from the outside, it boasted four bedrooms, a large kitchen and living room combo, and two bathrooms. Why did it remind me of a hospital? Dad had left some lamps lit offering a "welcome home" glow, but the place felt cold. Then I noticed the floors in every room. No hardwood, no carpet, just gray and white linoleum.

Gray.

Hospitals.

Linoleum.

Hospitals.

Welcome home.

Yeah, right.

"What do you think of the place?" Daddy asked.

How could I put this so as not to hurt his feelings?

"It's wonderful, dear," Mom said.

Oh. He hadn't been asking me.

Mom wrapped her arms around him and kissed his cheek. "It looks like there will be enough space for all of us." She gave him another kiss. "But we'd be happy to live in a one-room shack as long as you're there with us."

I didn't want a one-room shack. I didn't even want this four-bedroom, sterile house. "Could we buy a couple of rugs?"

"I don't think you'll want that," Daddy said. "On hot days, this floor will feel great under bare feet. Besides." He winked at Mom. "Tarantulas and scorpions hide easier in rugs and carpet."

Not funny.

Paul grabbed a Matchbox car from his knapsack. After placing it on the floor, he sent it rolling down the hall at top speed. "We're gonna set new records for distance here."

"Yeah, new records," Wade echoed.

Why couldn't I see the possibilities? Why did I have to wallow in memories of the gray hospital? I needed to change my attitude. In what corner of this place could I see something positive?

With one arm still wrapped around Mom, Daddy watched me. He knew. He knew I hated this place. He held out his free hand. A supplication? An invitation? The twinkle in his light blue eyes turned on before his lips turned up.

And there was the positive "something" I'd been searching for. Mom had known all along. I could live anywhere if Daddy lived there, too.

I returned his smile. The glow from the lamp intensified its warmth. The whirr of Matchbox wheels on tiled floors sounded just like they did back in our home on the base in New York. This would be my new home. For four months. And then? Another new home back in the same New York town. But would that really be home? Daddy wouldn't be there.

His smile faded. Had mine? We stared at each

other for an immeasurable moment. He knew what he was asking of us, what all soldiers asked of their families. Jimmy Pulizzi's face flashed into my mind. The stoic sadness when he told me *his* dad was going to Vietnam. I hoped his dad was still alive. I hoped Jimmy was doing okay in Queens at his grandma's. His plan of survival included learning all the bus routes in New York City.

Good soldiers always evaluated their situation and made a plan. Daddy and I had talked about that before he left for California. As long as I had a plan of action, I would be okay, too.

Daddy squeezed my hand. I didn't remember grasping it when he stretched it toward me. "You got a plan in place yet?" Amazing, how he could read my mind.

"I'm working on it," I said. "I need to check out the school first."

After we made several trips from the house to the car and back with all the luggage and odds and ends, Daddy gave us the grand tour. Krista and I each had our own bedroom. Nice for my privacy, but I'd miss her. Some of my friends would never admit that about *their* sisters. I'd be glad to have *my* sister back with me when we moved home again.

Krista, wide awake since our arrival, inspected her room. She gave me a questioning look when she saw the crib and dresser but no twin bed. I could tell she was wondering, *"Where is Debbie's bed?"* I led her to the room next door.

"My room." I pointed to myself. We walked back to her door. "Your room." I pointed to her.

Krista scowled, creating a little wrinkle between

her eyes. She pulled on my hand, and we walked to the middle of her room.

"Dah," she said.

That could mean anything. In this case, I knew she wanted us to be together, like usual.

I unpacked her suitcase, found some pajamas, and got her dressed for bed. "Let's say 'night-night' to Mommy and Daddy, and you go to sleep."

I carried her to the kitchen where Mom was rearranging cupboards to her liking.

"Krista's all ready for bed. Shall I put her down?"

"Thank you, Debbie." Mom smiled at us. Krista smiled back. "Did you brush her teeth?"

"Um, no."

Mom nested two fry pans in a lower cupboard. "I'll do it. And I'll take her to her room. I don't know how she'll handle this."

While I returned to my room to unpack, Krista protested over her new sleeping quarters by kicking the slats of her crib. Mom left her there to wail.

Ten minutes passed with no let-up. "Would you let her stay in my bed?" I asked. "Then we can put her back in the crib once she's asleep."

"Anything's worth a try at this point," Daddy grumbled.

Mom carried Krista to my room. Krista pointed at me.

"Yes." I pointed to myself. "My room."

Krista sniffled one last time, turned onto her side, and closed her eyes. Mom flipped the light switch, and we tiptoed into the hall. I don't know why we *tiptoed*. Krista couldn't hear us.

Chapter 6:
Sleepless in the Desert

This is a bad house.
Deh-bee is a bad girl, too.
She wants her own room.

On Tuesday morning to celebrate our arrival, Daddy made his Saturday special of pancakes and sausage. Mom just doesn't have the touch. Having waited a whole month to see him again, Dad's perfectly fluffy pancakes dripping with butter and syrup satisfied far more than my stomach.

After we ate, Mom didn't even ask me to wash up. We had an electric dishwasher! She shooed us out to explore the neighborhood leaving her free to set up her new household with the least amount of interruptions.

"You're not on a base anymore," she reminded us.

Translation: don't cut through the neighbors' yards.

When we lived on a base, no one cared about that. Everybody shared.

"And don't walk too far out in the desert. Keep the house in sight."

The boys immediately sprinted for the open desert behind the house across the street. Stepping gingerly out the front door, I checked for any poisonous spiders that might be crossing the concrete path between me and the driveway, then surveyed my surroundings as I followed the path. So, this was Masterville, in the Mojave Desert, in the Rockies, specifically, near the San Gabriel Mountains. I'd studied a little bit about western US geography, but living it was nothing like imagining it. Distant piles of stones surrounded me. An endless gravel pit.

The desert lay at my door, teeming with dangerous creatures. I sure couldn't run around barefoot in the sand. Not like at the beach. If something venomous didn't bite me, the heat from the ground would blister the soles of my feet.

A light, dusty breeze brushed my face, but no sound accompanied it. No trees with leaves existed so no leaves could whisper secrets to each other. Every door to every house remained shut. No cars rolled up and down the street in front of me. Only the distant screech of a hawk circling high in the azure sky broke the silence.

Our house was a yellow-beige, stucco-covered cube, one of hundreds built into the side of a steep sandy hill. Every block contained a series of terraces, each house and yard one step in the series. Ours blended in with the sand encircling the house. The tan cube next door boasted a rock garden with a cactus plant at its center. Nobody had grass. In fact, nothing was green at all except for an occasional scrubby tree or cactus.

I hated it.

"Debbie!" Mom's voice carried out the front door. "Take Krista with you."

With me *where*? I wasn't about to trail my brothers into the desert.

I trudged up the sidewalk holding Krista's hand. And *up* the sidewalk was the exact description as we took on a very steep hill. The houses varied in color from hospital gray to rose beige as if the builders wanted to camouflage them within the desert. One neighbor had painted some large rocks in neon colors. Too fake.

Meanwhile, Krista kept stopping to examine cracks in the sidewalk, bugs crawling in the sand along the concrete, or stones within her reach. I didn't let her touch the bugs or stick her fingers into the cracks. Could scorpions hide in there?

That night, Krista was still awake when Daddy came to move her to the crib so I could sleep. One look at him and she knew. Her screams sent me back to the living room.

She may have allowed herself to be tucked into my bed earlier, but she wasn't about to fall for the "*sleep* in Debbie's bed" routine again. Waking us at dawn with angry screeches, her opinion of our deception from the night before had come close to deafening the *rest* of the family.

"What do we do now?" I asked Mom. "I won't get any sleep."

Paul, Wade, and I were never allowed to have the temper tantrums Krista got away with. Our behinds received painful consequences for that kind of behavior. But we all made allowances for how frustrated Krista got when she couldn't understand what we said or why we did something. Which was most of the time.

However. She understood where her own bed was.

Mom put down her magazine, and we joined Daddy in my room. They regarded Krista, worried frowns on their faces, and then stared at each other. Without saying a word, they came to a decision together.

Daddy laid a gentle hand on my shoulder. "Get into bed with Krista. We'll pick her up once she's asleep."

Mom scooted Krista to one side of the bed. "She's got to be exhausted at this hour. She'll probably fall asleep quickly."

As soon as I pulled the sheet over both of us, Krista's screams stopped. She smiled and popped her thumb in her mouth. Her one crossed eye rolled closer to her nose, an obvious sign of how tired she was. Sure enough, Krista conked out within two minutes, and Daddy carried her to the next room.

Wednesday night, she perfected her bedtime recipe. Kick, scream, wail, look pathetic. Repeat until one parent tucks her into Debbie's bed. Stay awake, even when Debbie goes to bed. Stay awake until Mom and Daddy go to bed.

I dozed off while she was still kicking my back. The bedside clock read midnight when Daddy tried to take her to the crib. Krista woke up the whole house. Her feet shot out in every direction. Daddy wrapped his arms around her like a straitjacket, his lips in a grim, tight line.

Paul and Wade filled the doorway. Neither one of them looked very happy either.

"What's the big deal about her sleeping in her own

room?" This from Wade who had shared a room with Paul his entire life.

"When I was little and I kicked and screamed like that, you spanked me." Could Paul remember back that far?

"Let her stay with Debbie just for tonight," Mom pleaded. "We need our sleep."

Daddy blew out a sharp sigh. "Just for tonight."

"What? No! *I* won't get any sleep."

"One more night, Debbie." His voice let me know any further argument was pointless. "But we've got to figure out something. At this point, we're spoiling her."

He leaned down until Krista hovered a couple of inches above the mattress, then dropped her onto my bed. Without a smile for his darling little daughter, he strode out of the room. The boys shuffled back to theirs.

On my side with my elbow for support, I glowered at her, purposely giving her my witchy look. "You are *bad*." And I used the sign for that word. "I don't want you in my bed."

I had never turned that ugly look on my baby sister before. Krista's eyes rounded and her lower lip trembled. Before that innocent face could make me feel more guilty, I flipped over to my other side, ignoring her little fingers brushing my shoulder.

On Thursday morning, as Mom and I carried garbage cans to the curb for trash pick-up, I asked, "Don't people ever go outside here?"

Our neighbors still seemed nonexistent. Cars rolled up and down the street occasionally, but I'd never seen one person outside. No kickball games. No one watered their lawns—but then again, why would anybody water sand? People could at least take a walk. The days weren't all that hot in March.

Mom shrugged. "A lot of people are probably on vacation. We came during spring break, so you wouldn't miss any school."

I gazed up and down the silent street. 'Not everybody's on vacation. There are plenty of cars in the driveways."

As we walked toward the garage, a pick-up truck in need of a muffler drove up the hill past the front of our house. Mom waved. The driver didn't.

"Did you see that? She didn't even wave back to you. That's just rude."

Mom put her arm around my waist and drew me to her. "Daddy warned me we might not be welcome. Air Force families come and go all the time. They know we won't be staying long, so they're not interested in getting to know us."

"How come we've moved twelve times, and this is the first time no one wants to be friends just because we'll move again soon?"

"This time we're not on a base." Mom toted one more trash can to the curb. "When you're Air Force, you're used to moving, and you want to make friends wherever you can and for as long as you have. Civilians don't understand."

"We lived with civilians in Syracuse." I smashed the lid down on the over-full trash can trying to get it to stay shut. "We had plenty of friends there. And when we go back to Hampton Shores, we'll live off-base."

"We stayed in Syracuse for two *years*," Mom pointed out. "I don't know if we would have been welcomed if our neighbors knew we were leaving in less than six months. Same goes for Hampton Shores."

No. She was wrong. My friends back home would never abandon me. Missing Chip and Melissa and Leigh, I held a pity party while Paul and Wade rode their bikes up and down the streets and came back with a couple of kids they met at the elementary school playground.

Where were the junior high kids? Not on a playground, that's for sure.

Chapter 7:
Guilty Victory

Everyone is mean.
Deh-bee tricked me. Mah-mi and
Da-di made me cry.

On Thursday night, I dragged my mattress into Krista's room.

"What are you doing?" Mom emerged from the bathroom with a towel-wrapped Krista.

"I am not sharing my bed with her again." I pointed to the bratty little pixie in her arms.

After a sleepless night of kicks and pokes from bony little knees and elbows, any shame I'd felt about my awful words to her had flitted away with dawn's sparrows. Not that I'd noticed any sparrows in this place.

The same witchy look I used on Krista must have been on my face because Mom didn't argue. She could pull rank and force me to put the mattress back, but the whole family knew you didn't try to reason with Debbie when she wore The Look. My sleepless nights were officially over. Or else.

"Krista can go to sleep in her crib. I'll lie down on the mattress. Once she's asleep, I'll move the mattress back to my room."

Mom considered for a moment, then nodded in agreement. "It's worth a shot."

She dressed Krista in her pajamas and a double-thick diaper for overnight. Then she set Krista in the crib.

"You sleep here." She pointed to Krista, then the crib mattress, and made the sign we used for sleeping, hands in a prayer position tucked against her cheek.

"Debbie sleeps there." She pointed to me, my mattress, and repeated the sleep sign.

Krista's mouth drooped down. She watched me out of the corner of her left eye. I don't think she believed Mom, but she didn't cry when we kissed her goodnight and left the room. She was still awake, though, when I came to bed.

As long as she was up, I turned on the light. I inspected every corner of the room. I checked under the crib. The space was filled with shadow, and I couldn't see clearly. I'd forgotten a flashlight. I even lifted up my mattress, just in case something crawled under there. Krista watched my movements with high interest.

Satisfied I'd done my best, I turned out the light and tried to get comfortable. I sent up a prayer that no black widows would wander out from some crack between the floor and the wall and pay a visit to my mattress before I could drag it back to my room in the next half hour.

The next thing I knew, it was Friday morning. Krista stood in her crib, her smile proclaiming delight that I was still there. I lifted her out of bed, and we headed for the kitchen. No one else seemed to be up yet. I stuck Krista in her highchair and poured a bowl of Oatie Os for her and one of Rice Puffs for me. Once the clink of glass hit the counter, the boys were at my elbow. I handed over two more bowls.

Mom entered, tying her robe. She headed for the coffeepot, not the cereal. "Oh, it felt good to get some sleep."

I glared at her. "Why didn't you get me up and let me go back to my room?"

"You were sleeping so peacefully on the floor, I didn't want to wake you."

"I could've woken to scorpions all over me!"

She corrected my English. "Wakened."

"Woken. Wakened. I don't care. I just wanted to be alive in the morning." She needed to know I would *not* put up with Krista for one more night. "I am not sleeping on the floor again."

"Remember, it was your idea." She smirked at me. Infuriating.

On Friday night, my mattress was still on the floor. Krista relaxed when she saw all was set up like the night before, so she fell asleep right away. I dragged the mattress back to my room and slept until the middle of the night. That's when she woke up and realized I wasn't with her. Once again, her wailing didn't let any of us get rest.

Mom and Daddy didn't make me haul the mattress back to Krista's room, and they didn't let Krista out of bed no matter how loud she screamed or how hard she cried. They took turns for a while, telling her to go to sleep, but they didn't spank her. Finally, they shut her door and let her scream. My last glance at the alarm clock told me it was three-twelve in the morning before I passed out from exhaustion. Krista was still wailing.

On Saturday, I finally saw a boy about my age hovering over a bicycle. I walked down the hill to where his house stood on the corner lot, and I stopped a few yards from where he was applying a wrench to something on the handlebars. "Hi."

He squatted to fiddle with the bike pedals. "Hi."

Now what should I say? All I could see of the guy was the back of his not-so-white T-shirt, the seat of his blue jeans, and an extremely short haircut. Even my brothers wore theirs longer.

"What's wrong with your bike?"

"Nuthin's wrong with it. I took it apart. Now I'm putting it back together."

"Just for the fun of it?"

He twisted his neck to look at me, an annoyed frown on his face. The motion reminded me of an owl. "Yeah. Just for the fun of it. Is that such a surprise?"

I'd already messed up. "I don't know. I always thought people who are good with machines like to *fix* stuff. I never thought about them breaking it just so they *could* fix it."

He continued to stare at me, saying nothing.

Yeah, I'd made things worse, but that didn't stop me from pushing my foot farther into my mouth. "I'm terrible at fixing things, so I just…wouldn't know…" My voice trailed off, and I turned away in defeat, prepared to walk back up the hill.

"I'm Harvey."

I pivoted to face him. "I'm Debbie. I just moved in. Second house up the hill."

"Yeah, I know." He grinned. Gray eyes, straight white teeth, and a strong jaw made him almost handsome—if it weren't for the crew-cut.

"I met your brothers yesterday."

"Oh? They didn't tell me."

His grin widened. "They made sure to let me know you're a real sissy about the desert."

Thanks, guys. I lifted one shoulder just a smidge, hoping that looked cool. "Too many poisonous creatures crawling around. I'd be an idiot to go out there."

He glanced at my bare legs and sandaled feet. "You go out in those clothes, you sure would be an idiot. Wear sneakers. Better yet, boots."

"I've only got sneakers."

He was wearing boots and heavy denim dungarees in his own driveway. Maybe I shouldn't have walked down here. Could some rattlesnake jump out at me from anywhere? I peered across Harvey's yard.

Harvey—the guy who could twist his neck like an owl—hooted. Yes, he *hooted* at me. "You're lookin' for some critter right now, aren't you?"

"You're the one wearing boots." I bit out the words like a snapping turtle.

He grabbed a rag off the handlebars and wiped the grease from his hands. "Your brothers also said you were quiet and shy. Guess they were wrong."

How could I feel humiliated and flattered at the same time?

Harvey stepped over to a little motor scooter and patted the seat. "Why don't you come with me some time?"

"Out in the desert?"

"I'll show you there's nuthin' to be scared of."

"There are snakes and scorpions out there, right?" I waved my hand toward the barren expanse across the street.

His superior grin was maddening. "Sure there are. Just wear sneakers and jeans, and as long as you don't do something dumb like stick your hand under a rock, there's no danger."

Stick my hand under a rock. How dumb did he think I was? I gazed at the expanse of wilderness across the road. Would I dare to go out there? On a motorcycle? With a guy I barely knew?

"If you know what you're doing, then yeah, I'd like to explore it a little."

"If I know what I'm doing." He grunted and returned to tinkering with his bicycle.

Harvey didn't compare to Chip back home, but at least I had one friend now. Maybe.

Saturday night, Mom put Krista in her crib. My mattress remained on my own bed. Krista whimpered. Mom gave her a kiss and tucked her in. I kissed her, too. Krista pointed to the wall that divided our two rooms.

I nodded and pointed to her. "You sleep here." I made the sleep sign. Then I pointed to myself, made the sleep sign again, and pointed to the wall. "And I sleep over there."

Tears filled her eyes, and guilt almost sent me to

my room for the mattress. Mom nipped that idea quick. She kissed Krista again and waved bye. "See you in the morning." Taking firm hold of my arm, she led me out. At the door, I turned and signed, "I love you."

"Debbie." Mom batted down my hand. "Stop it. Just say the words."

The doctors had told us to only use speech with Krista. Otherwise, she would never learn English. But Krista didn't know many words, and we didn't understand what she wanted.

If Mom saw me using signs, like just now, she got mad. I was making the problem "worse." Maybe. Maybe not. Anyway, why should I listen to what the doctors said? I knew Krista was deaf before they did.

Mom headed toward the kitchen while I pretended to go to my room. As soon as she was out of sight, I returned to Krista's door. I blew her a kiss, and in defiance of doctors everywhere, signed, "I love you." She didn't sign back, but knelt in her crib, hands gripping the bars, so sad.

When I peeked in half an hour later, little snores and snuffles met my ears. I leaned in to kiss her cheek but decided I'd better not. The slightest touch might wake her. Inhaling the sweet scent of baby shampoo, I noticed she had silently cried herself to sleep. Her cheeks were still wet.

Mom, Dad, and I may have won the bedroom war, but victory was not sweet.

Chapter 8:
Sunday Morning

We all get dressed up
Like we are going to church.
Is there a new church?

Finally able to sleep the whole night, I woke at sunrise. No one else seemed to be up. No clatter from the kitchen, no hum of voices on the television. I peered out my window. From behind a distant mountain peak, the sun rose. I couldn't help but think of the song from years of music classes. "O beautiful for spacious skies... For purple mountain majesties..."

The mountain *was* purple. It *was* full of majesty. In daylight, it looked like a pile of rubble, but right now, it...was regal. And...awesome. Something inside my chest swelled to the point that I thought I might burst. And if I did explode from that pressure, I knew it would feel glorious. All I wanted to do was praise God. A blast of exultation.

I guess I'd been feeling like God didn't care about me anymore, making me move away from my friends, sending me to a place painted in ugly browns and grays, taking my dad away from me for a whole year. But He'd just proved to me how wrong I was. He'd given me my very own beautiful mountain. Every time I looked out this window at sunrise, I wanted to remember He was still there for me. No matter where I lived.

Looking at least sixteen in my sunshine yellow dress and my white spike heels, I pranced out the front door on my way to the car. Daddy's eyebrows rose to his hairline when he glanced at my feet. He wouldn't make me put on flat shoes, would he? I offered what I hoped was a perky smile. No smile in return, but he didn't order me back to the house either. I slid into the car, smoothing my dress under my behind so it wouldn't wrinkle.

As he buckled his seat belt, Daddy muttered under his breath. "I'm not sure I'm ready for the next few years."

Mom, with her perfume and make-up and aqua linen suit that fit her every curve, looked ten times more attractive than me. She placed a sympathetic hand on his shoulder. "Don't worry. She'll always be your little girl." She kissed his cheek, then looked my way, her eyes still containing a tender glow.

I was all jumbled inside. I liked looking older than thirteen, and while I'd never admit it out loud, I liked being the apple of my father's eye. He would always see me as his little girl, and that was good.

Our tiny car putt-putted its way to Apple Valley

where we stopped at a small church with a Spanish-mission look to it, built of stucco and painted white. Arched windows were cut into the walls, and a red-tiled roof added much needed color to its desert surroundings. It was pretty. The lady who had parked next to us greeted us with a "hello" and a smile. Before we reached the church doors, several others shook hands with my parents, said "hi" to me and my brothers, and cooed over Krista. At least *some* people were friendly in California.

Paul and Wade followed Dad to their Sunday school classrooms, and I went with Mom and Krista to the nursery. All the younger kids' rooms were in a separate building. Krista's was full of light with plenty of toys, and a gentle, smiling teacher. With only four other toddlers in her class, Mrs. Wilson made a big fuss over her new charge.

Krista examined several brightly colored blocks and didn't seem to notice when Mom left, dragging me with her. I wanted to stay in this safe, cozy room as a teacher's aide instead of facing the junior high class in the main building. I might have appeared to be a confident teenager on the outside, but in my mind, I was an awkward little kid stumbling around like a doofus. Would anybody talk to me? Would I meet a pack of wolves or a kennel filled with friendly puppies when I got to the youth Sunday school room?

As we crossed a courtyard with an artfully-designed cactus garden, we passed by a good-looking blond guy with glasses. I sneaked a peek backward. He was staring at me. A blush heated my neck and cheeks. He grinned, then continued in the opposite direction. I smiled the rest of the way to my classroom.

My Sunday School teacher introduced himself. "Good morning! I'm Merle Finch." He shook my hand.

"Nice to meet you, Mr. Finch."

"Call me Merle." I wasn't sure my parents would agree with that, but he kept talking, not waiting for my response. "You're Grant Hansen's daughter, right? He told me the family would be with him today. Welcome. Help yourself to a doughnut."

A couple of the kids said "hi", but nobody introduced themselves, and Merle didn't do the honors. Comforted by the sweet glaze on my doughnut, I sat on a metal folding chair and stared at the blank walls while Merle taught the day's lesson, something to do with how fickle people are. One week they're cheering Jesus as the king, the next, bellowing, "Crucify him." Or was he talking about two different sets of people? Not wanting to be the *stupid* new girl, I didn't ask any questions.

After class and back in the desert heat, alone, the blond guy stepped to my side. "Hi again." He dazzled me with a movie star smile boasting straight white teeth. "I'm Bryce."

Ooooh. And a movie star-sounding name, too. It took me a second to remember my own.

"Um, I'm Debbie."

Except for the glasses, Bryce could be part of the cast for a Frankie Avalon surfside movie. "You're from New York, aren't you? How do you like it on the West Coast?"

"How do you know I'm from New York?"

"I met your dad last Sunday. He told me."

My dad had gotten awfully talkative. First Merle, now Bryce.

Bryce scanned the courtyard. "And since you're the only new girl I've seen today, you must be his daughter."

His intense gaze examined me as if I were some rare specimen. The never-before-seen-but-often-heard-of New York City Babe. Like I'd labeled him the Dreamy California Surfer Guy. I don't know how long we stood there gazing into each other's eyes. Too afraid of saying something dumb, I didn't utter a word.

Bryce broke the silence. "I noticed you in the parking lot. Why does your little sister walk on her toes?"

Wasn't it rude to blurt out a question about a person's physical problems? But the guy had a knack for making me feel special, like "I noticed you in the parking lot."

"Krista has cerebral palsy. Her legs are spastic which means her muscles are too tight. Did you ever wear braces on your teeth?" So there. See if he liked some bad manners thrown at him.

He flashed those pearly whites, not at all insulted. "Yeah. Got them off a month ago."

What a flirt. We reached the steps of the church where Mom and Dad waited.

"See you later." Bryce nodded to my parents then ran up the steps into church.

Daddy grinned down at me. "A conquest already?"

Apparently, he was quickly getting used to his grown-up daughter.

"Oh, stop it," Mom scolded. "She's boy-crazy enough already!"

"You were crazy about me in fifth grade, and you know it." Daddy always teased her about their lifelong romance.

I ignored them. Sundays were going to be my favorite day of the week.

Chapter 9:
School in the Desert

Oh, no. 'Ool again.
Deh-bee, Paw, and Way leave me.
Wait. There is a pool?

On Monday, I started the dreaded, mile-long walk down the mountain to the junior high school. Alone. Paul and Wade's elementary school was only a few blocks *up* the mountain. They could face any challenge together, but I felt like one lone captive forced to run between two lines of enemy warriors. Everybody would be checking out my weaknesses. The bullies would strike while others would wait and see if I survived before making any moves to help.

Too bad Bryce and I didn't go to the same school, but Daddy said he lived in Apple Valley. Having his smooth confidence standing next to me would've boosted mine. Mom offered to drive me, but I turned her down. A person entering school with their *mother* could end up with a ruined reputation before they even made it to their first class. I figured a trip to the guidance office to get a class schedule should be easy enough to accomplish by myself.

The mountain's morning air was clean, cool, and silent. Not a dog barked, not a bird called. My light jacket over a short-sleeved sweater kept me warm. The sky, bright blue and cloudless, would call up the dust by afternoon. Didn't it ever rain here? *That's why it's called a desert, Debbie.*

I passed Harvey's house, hoping he might walk with me, but his bike was already missing from the open garage. For each block down the hill, the houses got shabbier. Cracks created spider web designs on the walls, and crumbling stucco made for uneven patches, especially around the corners of window frames. Porches sagged under the weight of washing machines and cast-off couches. In spite of their run-down condition, these homes were prettier than the cubes on my street. Hanging flowerpots with cascades of color displayed defiance in the face of poverty.

A girl with long black hair walked slowly ahead of me. Her sneakers scuffed the loose pebbles causing them to rattle down the hill. Maybe she was in the junior high.

"Hi," I said as I came alongside her.

Fear lurked in her eyes. Or was that my imagination? How could I possibly scare anyone?

"Hi," she said in almost a whisper.

"Is this the right way to the junior high?"

"Yes." Her voice was only slightly louder.

"Oh, good. I wasn't sure." A white lie. "Is it okay if I walk with you?"

Again, the startled look followed by a hushed reply. "I guess so."

"My name's Debbie."

A hesitation. "I'm Mara."

"What grade are you in?"

"Eighth."

"I'm in seventh."

I wasn't the chatty type, but Mara was so quiet, I needed to fill the silence with something. "I moved here last week. From New York. California is so different. I mean, you've got flowers blooming on all the porches already, and back home we don't even have leaves on the trees. What do you call the bush with the white flowers? They smell wonderful."

She stared at me for a moment as if trying to figure out why this babbling stranger wouldn't leave her alone.

"They're called mock orange."

At least I think that's what she said. Her voice was still too quiet, and she turned away as she spoke.

"Yeah, they do remind me of orange blossom cologne." I inhaled. "Mmmmm."

We reached the bottom of the hill, turned a corner, and the school sprawled below us on the edge of town. It was different from any school I'd ever seen, and I'd seen a lot of schools.

Terra Playa Junior High School wasn't just one large building. A double row of low rectangular structures, like stucco longhouses, surrounded each side of a huge cube of cement blocks. Concrete paths connected all of them and crisscrossed the open area in between the longhouses and the central building. I'd never attended a school where I went outside to change classes. Intriguing. Flowering shrubs lined the paths, and *grass* grew in the open spaces, the first true lawn

I'd seen in a week.

Mara pointed me to the main office then took off without a "goodbye" or a "see you around."

Figuring out my schedule was easier than I'd hoped, and the guidance counselor introduced me to Bryce's female equivalent in Californian good looks. Pam would help me find my classrooms. She and I had the same schedule except for the last hour where she took French, and I took Spanish. At lunch time, everybody ate outside, and she invited me to sit with her and a group of friends. What a relief not to sit by myself.

Weathered picnic tables filled the courtyard, and the breeze carried the scent of something spicy from the cafeteria inside the large central building. A line of kids waiting to buy lunch snaked its way from the doors to the far side of the commons area.

I pulled out my peanut butter and jelly sandwich. "What happens when it rains?"

"Hardly ever happens," Pam replied.

"There are places to sit inside," said a beautiful girl with gorgeous golden-brown hair flowing down her back.

While the girls nearest to me pointed out the cutest guys in our class, Mara walked past our table.

I smiled and waved. "Hi, Mara."

She jerked her head around to see who spoke. Nodding to me, she scurried toward a group of Mexican-American kids. Why was she so spooked?

"How do you know *her*?" Pam asked, her eyes following Mara's retreat.

"I met her on the way to school today. She's awfully shy."

"Just stay away from her, okay?"

"Really?"

Mara didn't seem like the type to offer me a cigarette or anything.

"We don't talk to girls like her."

The eyes that scared off Mara drilled into me.

"Why not?"

The girl with magnificent hair looked shocked at my simple question. Other girls ruined their perfect features with frowns of disgust or glares of horror as if I had insulted Mother Teresa or something.

"Because they're *Chicanos*." Pam spit out the words like an impatient mother instructing her stupid child to look both ways before crossing the street.

"You mean, you don't have anything to do with them because they're Mexican?" I had Puerto Rican friends in New York. Was I supposed to stay away from them, too?

"Chicano," Pam corrected me. "We call them Chicano."

She made *Chicano* sound nasty like when Mom teaches Krista that poop is *ca-ca* stinky.

One of the other girls added, "We stay away from them, and they stay away from us."

"That's ridiculous." The words popped out of my mouth before I could think to keep them inside.

Eyes glittered with either hot fury or cold contempt. Lips tightened to grim lines or curled into sneers. Pam didn't escort me to any of my afternoon classes. And Miss Gorgeous Hair glowered at me throughout sixth period choir after the director complimented my singing.

Instead of gaining a new group of friends, I'd made

a bunch of enemies. And I wouldn't be welcomed by the Mexican—Chicana—girls either. A desert of my own making.

Chapter 10:
Desert Blossoms

No-wah-een. My friend.
Curly hair, gray eyes, big smile.
I love No-wah-een.

I t's true. First impressions last.

Those girls never spoke to me again. But they spoke to a lot of other people and spread the word about the new white girl who liked Chicanos. *Nobody* talked to me.

On Friday, I sat at an empty lunch table. One more afternoon to endure, and my first excruciating, long week at this school would be over.

A girl with unfashionably short, nut-brown, corkscrew curls set her lunch tray opposite mine. I'd noticed her earlier in the week when a teacher had grabbed her arm before her fist went flying into another kid's face. Was I her next victim?

"Hey," she said as she plopped onto the bench.

"Hi." My voice sounded too high. Like the scared mouse that I was.

"You're new. Where you from?" She took a giant

bite of burrito.

"New York."

Her eyebrows rose while she chewed on her mouthful. Once she swallowed most of it, she said, "So you're the one that has the Staaaahlings in meltdown." Her voice mimicked Mrs. Thurston Howell the Third from *Gilligan's Island*. The millionaire's wife.

"The *Staaaah*lings?" Was that the name of a prominent family around here?

"Mmm-hmm. They *think* they're Hollywood 'starlets,' and they *are* the little 'darlings' of their mothers. Put 'em together, and all you've got is a plain, old, common bird."

I relaxed and ventured a grin as I got her play on words. Pam and her flock fit the title. If this rough-and-tough girl disliked them, I was safe. *For now.*

"Mmm-hmm." She took another bite and chose not to talk with her mouth full.

I opened my twin pack of orange cupcakes and offered her one.

She grinned. A little bit of brown paste stuck to her chipped, front tooth. "Thanks."

"You're welcome."

She coughed a laugh as she set the cupcake on her tray. "Gets the Starlings all atwitter, and she's polite, too."

I waited silently, unsure how to respond.

"I think I'll call you 'High Society,' like *New Yohk* high society, y'know?" She had a skill for mimicry. Now she sounded like she was born in the Bronx.

I shrugged. "Or you could call me Debbie."

"Debbie? Okay." With the burrito in one hand, she eyed the cupcake, like she couldn't decide whether to save it for dessert or not. "I'm Nora Jean."

Decision made, she snatched up the cupcake. With one bite, almost half of it disappeared. She rolled her eyes in ecstasy. "Ohhh, that's good. I haven't had one of these since I was little."

"They're my favorite, and as long as I eat a healthy lunch with it, my mom keeps buying them."

She stopped chewing and stared hard at me. Couldn't a seventh-grader even *mention* the word "mom" in California?

She finished the cupcake before saying, "So what does *your* mom insist is healthy?"

"Fruits and vegetables…meat…potatoes?"

"Huh. That doesn't sound too bad. My foster mother says healthy food is stuff like celery and spinach. Green things." Nora Jean returned to her burrito.

"But burritos aren't green."

"What she don't know, won't hurt her. Or me." She wolfed down the rest of the tortilla.

Nora Jean walked home with me and enjoyed another healthy snack of sliced apples at our kitchen table.

"Are you in any of Debbie's classes?" Mom asked.

"No, ma'am. We just have the same lunch hour."

"Nora Jean's in eighth grade," I added.

Mom looked puzzled. She'd been hounding me to *be friendly,* and now I could only find a friend from a different class? She just didn't get it.

Nora Jean handed Krista a piece of apple. Krista smiled and offered one of her own slices off of the highchair tray, now slimy with apple pulp.

Nora Jean beamed right back at her. "Thank you."

Her fingers closed over the slice, and she pressed her closed fist against her mouth, then nodded in appreciation.

Delighted, Krista handed her another.

"No, no. You keep it. I have some right here." She pointed to her plate using her other hand.

She popped one of her own apple slices into her mouth. From my vantage point next to her, I could see the results of her sleight-of-hand as she dropped Krista's slice out of her fist and into the paper napkin on her lap.

Hard to believe it was the same fist that almost got her suspended from school.

After Mom wiped Krista's sticky hands and face, Nora Jean and I took her outside. We examined the dirt and stones and the small flowers Mom had planted near the house,

"I've been walking with Krista around the front yard every day," I informed Nora Jean.

"Isn't that kind of boring?"

"Krista doesn't seem to think so. She's curious about everything."

"A happy, little sprite." Nora Jean grinned as Krista stuck her nose into one of Mom's flowers.

"Maybe a little too curious. She wants to touch bugs."

"That could be a problem."

I pulled Krista away from the blossom and checked to make sure no poisonous insects lurked in its center. "And we walk for the exercise, too." I pointed at the leg braces, heavy contraptions of leather and metal that continually stretched Krista's spastic muscles. "The sand forces her legs to work hard, and I'm hoping that will help strengthen them."

Nora Jean wrinkled her nose. "They look like torture devices."

They did. Steel rods reached almost to Krista's hips, and hinges at the knees allowed her legs to bend. Leather straps tied the rods together so her legs remained trapped between them. "Krista hates them."

"Do they hurt?"

Nora Jean's concern proved that this tough girl was not nearly as tough as I'd feared.

"No. They just slow her down. When she's not wearing them, she runs on tiptoe all the time. And she's got to get hot wearing those things all day in ninety degrees."

Krista used her arm to wipe a trickle of sweat off of her forehead.

Nora Jean handed her two pebbles. One was round, the other jagged.

Nora Jean pointed to the round, black stone. "Smooth." She stroked it.

Krista looked at the pebbles, dropped the jagged one, and copied Nora Jean's motion by petting the smooth one with a finger.

"Yes. Smooth." Nora Jean made sure Krista could see the shape of the word on her lips. Krista's mouth formed a silent "ooo."

Picking up the jagged stone again, Nora Jean handed it to Krista. "Rough."

With the smooth stone dropped and forgotten, Krista studied the second pebble, touching several pointy edges, then looked up to Nora Jean again.

"Rough." Nora Jean repeated the word. "Rough."

Krista copied Nora Jean so her front teeth rested on

her lower lip.

Nora Jean and I clapped our hands. Krista understood applause and grinned. However, a small prickly pear cactus growing on the edge of the property next to us claimed her attention. She ambled over to it and stretched one finger toward the spines, but I pulled her hand away.

"Sharp. Ow," I said, and shook my hand as though it hurt.

Krista frowned. She had just learned "smooth" and "rough." Which word fit this thing? She reached for the cactus again.

I pulled her hand away again. "No. It's sharp. Ow!"

She jabbered and shrieked at me.

Nora Jean laughed, exposing her chipped tooth. "We probably don't want to know what she's saying right now. Your mom would wash her mouth out with soap."

When Krista moved toward the plant again, I grabbed her hand and guided it toward one of the spines. Her finger barely touched it. With an expression of surprise, she jerked away and looked at me, a question in her eyes.

"Ow!" I said, and I shook my hand again.

Her lips formed the same shape as mine did. "Ow," she said clearly.

Nora Jean screamed in delight. "Her first word!"

As if Krista were her own sister.

Chapter 11:
Black Widow Boogie

Look at my spider.
Black with a red dot. Pretty!
But Way smashes it.

I dropped off Nora Jean at her house on my way up the hill. Wednesday was "Ironing Day." Nora Jean faced a pile of shirts to iron every week that would take me hours to finish. Mom never gave me that chore. Probably because all of our shirts would have burn marks on them. Nora Jean told me that if she gets any scorch marks on what she irons, then her foster mom won't even let her have salad dressing to put on all those greens she eats for dinner every night. Not for a whole week until the next ironing day.

That had to be some kind of child abuse.

I hadn't yet met this ogre of a woman who already reminded me of Cinderella's stepmother, but I would on Friday. Nora Jean had permission for me to come over that afternoon and stay for dinner. I wasn't sure I wanted to.

What if, like in the Hansel and Gretel fairy tale, the

foster mother locked me up where no one could find me, like in the basement or something? What if Nora Jean was in cahoots with her, so I would do all the housework and not her? How well did I know Nora Jean anyway?

But I needed to know the truth. Nora Jean claimed her foster mom did nothing around the house. Nora Jean did all the cooking and cleaning. Monday, bathrooms. Tuesday, laundry. Wednesday, ironing., Thursday, vacuuming. Friday, dusting. Saturday, changing the sheets. Sunday was the sabbath, and all they did was sit around the house with the shades closed against the sun. She could read the Bible or take a nap, but she couldn't watch television. Nora Jean made meat and potato dinners for the parents, but was only allowed green vegetables for herself.

Was Nora Jean exaggerating, outright lying, or was Mrs. Loughmiller as bad as Nora Jean made her out to be?

For now, my Wednesday afternoon would be spent walking Krista around the yard again. Once I changed into shorts, I took Krista outside. What would she discover today?

She immediately zeroed in on a sliver of green close to the stones and Mom's flowers wilting in the heat. A praying mantis sat perfectly still. Krista moved to touch it. I signed "no" and bit my finger, then pointed to the mantis. Krista's eyes widened in surprise, and she squatted to watch it.

He was at least four inches long, a beautiful spring green. Krista watched the mantis eat several bugs that wandered into its path. She leaned closer to watch him chew, but she didn't touch. She'd learned her lesson about touching critters and plants of the desert.

Maybe not.

On Thursday afternoon, Vacuum the House Day for Nora Jean, I didn't go out walking but chose to read in my room. I'd only gotten a couple of pages into the chapter when Mom screamed. Dropping my book, I beat a path to the kitchen. Krista stood smiling, palm open to share her great find, but Mom stood frozen, an expression of horror on her face. One look at Krista's treasure, and I screamed, which brought Wade inside to investigate. When he saw her offering, he joined the screams.

Krista held a black widow spider. We didn't dare move. If we hit it, it might bite us, or worse, bite Krista, which could kill her. The spider didn't move. Mom finally had the presence of mind to smack downward on Krista's hand so the awful thing fell to the floor. She stomped on it. We all stared at the dreaded creature.

Wade stomped it again for good measure. "Did it bite her?"

Mom inspected her hand. "Do you see any marks?"

Krista's eyes darted from one anxious face to another. She had been so pleased with her discovery, but no one else was happy about it. She set up a wail.

"Oh, no." Mom grabbed her purse from a chair. "She *is* hurt. We have to get to the hospital."

I started to object—we hadn't seen any puncture marks—but she whirled around the house in a panic, searching for car keys, for bacterial ointment, for matches. Matches? What does she want to do, burn the dead spider the way we flamed live ticks back on Long Island?

"Don't leave the house. I'll try to call your father from the clinic." She caught up Krista in her arms and rushed out the door.

Wade and I gazed down at the splattered black widow.

"How do we get it in the trash without touching it?" he asked.

"What about a paper towel?"

"I don't know." Wade peered closer at the smashed bug on our hospital gray floor. "It's got some guts squished out, and the paper towel will soak it up, and we might touch the wet part of the towel, and maybe the poison will get on our hands."

"Yeah, you might be right."

"What about aluminum foil? That doesn't soak up anything."

I shook my head. "Then the guts will slide around on the floor while we try to scoop up the body."

Wade nodded and frowned in thought. "We need something that can act like fingers."

A light bulb lit up in my brain. "How about tweezers?"

"Yeah, tweezers. I know where they are." He made a beeline for Mom and Dad's room.

He returned with the tweezers Mom used on her eyebrows. After carefully positioning the two pincers on either side of the spider's remaining leg, he squeezed, lifted the leg with what was left of the body dangling from it, and dropped it on the square of foil I had ready for him. We folded the foil over the corpse and crimped the edges tight. Wade buried it in the trash while I took a cotton ball soaked in rubbing alcohol and sterilized the tweezers, I hoped. The sharp scent of bleach filled the room as Wade washed the spot on the floor with scouring powder and a wet paper towel. Surely that bleach would protect him from any splatted venom.

Mom and Krista got home at the same time Daddy was dropped off from work and Paul returned from baseball practice. As she told us what happened at the hospital, Daddy's face turned pink. He wrapped one arm around her shoulders and made sure not to look at her. When he glanced at me, his eyes twinkled, he pressed his lips together, and his face deepened into a darker pink.

Mom shook her head. "I'm sure the hospital staff couldn't believe this dumb Easterner thought her child had been poisoned. They told me she would have cried as soon as it bit her. And I found out once it's dead, it's harmless."

"Well, everybody knows that," Paul said, scorn in his voice.

Wade and I looked at each other. The tweezer episode would remain our little secret.

Chapter 12:
Steaks for Dinner

Where is my sister?
Deh-bee did not eat dinner.
I hope she's okay.

I can't believe they're letting you come over." Nora Jean almost bounced with excitement. "They've never let me have a friend over before. But I really talked you up."

I'd only known her for a week, but I'd never seen Nora Jean happy and excited. At school, she wore a frown whenever I passed her in the crowd between classes, and at my house she was more relaxed, but I wouldn't say she was happy.

"Did you tell them I was related to the Queen of England or something?"

Nora Jean had told me Mrs. Loughmiller read every gossip paper on the British royals.

"Almost. I told them you weren't like other people I knew. You didn't smoke or drink. You made good grades in school. And you were polite."

"I can't believe I'm the first friend you've had with

those qualifications."

She turned to look at me as we stopped at a busy street corner. "See? What average bozo uses the word, 'qualifications?' And yeah, you're the first friend like that."

Back in New York, I knew kids in high school who smoked and drank, but hardly any of us in the junior high did. Did Nora Jean usually hang out with the potheads and partyers? Maybe even gang members?

The light turned green, and we crossed the street.

I had to ask. "So why did you sit at my table a week ago if all your other friends don't have those *qualifications?*"

We walked along a sidewalk that fronted dingy stucco homes and across the street from some kind of factory.

I thought she wasn't going to answer me, but she finally broke the silence. "If I can stay out of trouble for the next year, I'll be home free."

"What do you mean, *home free?*"

"I'll be sixteen, I can drop out of school and go live with my brother. I can put up with being a slave for just thirteen more months."

The not being a slave part of it sounded good to me, but dropping out of school was a bad idea. "How old is your brother? Where are you going to get money to live? Won't the Loughmillers call the police and bring you back?"''

She stopped short on the sidewalk and peered at me with the same hard expression she gave everyone when she stood in the lunch line. "You sound like somebody's grandma."

Maybe. But grandmas are usually right.

Nora Jean resumed her pace. "Look. Kase and I—Kase is my brother—we have a plan. He and a buddy live on the south side of town. They're twenty-one, and they have jobs at a service station. Kase said I can come live with them, get my own job, like a waitress or something. Then I can help with their rent, and I'll do whatever I feel like doing after work."

"And the Loughmillers won't care?"

"Huh." Her lip curled in a sneer. "They probably won't bother to let anyone know. Just keep taking the state's money."

This was going to be one weird evening. Or maybe I should beg off and go home. But I couldn't hurt Nora Jean's feelings. For all of her tough exterior, she reminded me of a helpless baby bird.

And she was kind. She'd adored my sister on sight. And she was willing to be a friend when no one else in the whole school would.

"But you're so good with Krista. I think you should stay in school and be a teacher."

"Ha! Me, a teacher?" She shook her head and pointed to the next corner. "Left, then right, then we're home, sweet home." The mockery didn't leave her voice when she added, "A teacher. I can just see it. 'Ms. Reilly, can I have a pass for the bathroom?' 'Ms. Reilly, I lost my pencil.' I'd be telling the kid to hold it like I had to, and I'd probably smack him for being an idiot who's not able to keep a pencil in his desk."

Maybe she was right. Nora Jean might have patience with Krista, but she didn't have patience with anyone else.

She turned a portion of her temper on me. "Besides, you need college to be a teacher. Where would I get the money for that, huh?"

I was back to being a scared mouse, but I screwed up enough courage to say, "You could get a scholarship."

Another sharp *ha*. "I get Cs and Ds. I don't think so.

"I could tutor you."

That shut her up. The hot glare cooled to something wistful. "You would, wouldn't you?"

"Yeah, I would. I like to teach."

"Except there's one problem. How are you going to tutor me after you go back to New York?"

It was my turn to have no good answer.

As we walked up to her front door, she tapped a gentle fist on the back of my head. "Don't worry about it. No scholarships for me. But I'll be fine."

I stepped into a small living room that reeked of cigarette smoke. The walls might have been white once, but they rippled between tan and gray. And the overstuffed mustard yellow sofa had seen better days. A portable television on a small stand sat opposite the sofa, and an upholstered wingback chair was positioned off to the side at an angle.

The chair's fabric boasted huge purple flowers blooming against the same mustard yellow background as the sofa. Sew a few honeybee appliqués to the petals, and Nora Jean had her very own psychedelic garden.

In contrast, her bland bedroom held only the basics. A twin bed, neatly made up with a white sheet and thin gray blanket. A small dresser, and a smaller desk.

She dumped her books on the desk, then spread out her arms. "My place."

I nodded.

"I'll get us some ice water, then I'll get going on the dusting, and you can watch TV until I'm done."

"You want me to help? It'll get done quicker." I hated to dust.

Her face lit up, then shadowed. "No, I'd better do it. Louise expects it done a certain way, and it would take longer to teach you than if I just do it myself." She gave me a hopeful look. "Would you do the hall bathroom?"

I'd rather clean toilets than dust, but--a stranger's toilet?

She must have seen the indecision on my face. "On Fridays, it's just making sure the sink and mirror are spot-free."

"Okay. I can do that." Armed with supplies, I marched to the bathroom.

It looked spotless to me. Not even a toothpaste tube took up space on the counter. A swipe of glass cleaner on the mirror. A just-to-make-sure squirt and wipe on the counters, and I was done. I even straightened the hand towels.

Nora Jean had turned on the TV and was watching *Dark Shadows* while she dusted. I retrieved my water and sat on the couch.

"Stan's got steaks in the fridge. For all *four* of us." She laughed. "Yeah, I guess they think you're royalty. They usually buy hamburger, or cheaper. And I won't be doing much cooking either. Stan is *The Man* when it comes to grilling."

So maybe Nora Jean *wasn't* forced to eat only green stuff all the time. Although she was certainly telling the truth about the household chores.

At five-thirty sharp, the front door opened. A rotund woman with upswept, dark brown hair stepped inside. Even shorter than Nora Jean, Mrs. Loughmiller glanced around the room with an intense look on her face before settling her focus on me. She rearranged her features into a feral smile, which along with her pointy eyeglasses, gave new meaning to the term *fat cat.*

"You must be Debbie. Nice to meet you."

"Nice to meet you, too."

She bustled past me into the kitchen before I finished my sentence.

Peering into the refrigerator, she asked, "Where's the salad? I left you a note."

Nora Jean ambled into the kitchen, winking as she passed me. "You left a note? I didn't see one."

Mrs. Loughmiller shut the refrigerator door and frowned at it. "I had the note taped to the door. Potatoes in the oven at five-fifteen and make a tossed salad."

Nora Jean shrugged. "I didn't see a note. Sorry." She turned to me. "Did you see a note?"

I hadn't been in the kitchen. "No."

She pointed to the stove. "Don't worry. I figured we always have baked potatoes with steak, so I put them in the oven a little after five. And since we have plenty of cans of beans and corn, I knew it wouldn't take long to heat up one of them."

Mrs. Loughmiller wouldn't let it go. "I *know* I taped a note."

"Maybe you only thought you taped it. You were in kind of a hurry this morning." With her foster mom still staring at the door, Nora Jean grinned at me, her eyes dancing with mischief.

If the Loughmillers were as mean as Nora Jean

made them out to be, she sure wasn't scared of them. Or maybe they were kind, and Nora Jean was the truly mean person. And if that were the case, what did she have in mind for *me*?

Mrs. Loughmiller clucked her tongue and turned away from the refrigerator. "At least the potatoes will be ready. Debbie, do you prefer beans or corn?"

Canned beans were mushy. Mom always bought the frozen kind. "Corn would be good."

I got the feeling Mrs. Loughmiller preferred corn over beans, too. In the tiny kitchen, she stood just a couple of feet away from me, and her magnified brown eyes warmed as they looked up at me. Even with her high heels, I was a good deal taller, although the height of her beehive hairdo got her to my five-foot-four.

"Perfect." She spun on one spiked heel to face her ward. "Steak, potatoes, and corn it is. Nora Jean, get two cans of corn."

"Oh, what's this?" Nora Jean pointed to a triangle barely visible under one corner of the refrigerator. She pulled on the triangle and out slid a note-sized scrap of paper with tape along one edge. "The note. It must have fallen off."

Mrs. Loughmiller's eyes hardened as she slowly pivoted to face her ward. Nora Jean hadn't fooled anybody.

Chapter 13:
Fragile Little Legs

I love the desert.
Rain falls on Deh-bee and me.
We dance and get wet.

I was ready to start exercise time on Tuesday night when Paul walked into Krista's bedroom. "Let me try it."

I wrinkled my nose and sniffed. "You stink."

Sweat and dirt tracked down his cheeks, and he trailed an odor like a gym locker full of dirty socks.

"So? I don't have to smell good to push on Krista's foot."

"Aren't you watching *The Green Hornet?*"

"Nah, some special news show is on. Boring."

I shrugged. "Go ask Mom if she'll let you."

He'd need a bath before she allowed him near Krista, who was already baby powder-fresh and her hair still damp from shampoo. She grinned at me as she sat in the crib and played with her giraffe.

Krista never had a tantrum about the leg exercises the way she did with the hearing aids. She seemed to know that stretching the calf muscles helped. Every night we ran through the routine, Mom, Daddy, or me. It was like placing your foot against a stair step, pressing on the step to flex your foot, and then bending your knee and leaning forward. It felt good—up to a point. We were supposed to take Krista just past the "feel-good" point, three or four times with each foot.

Krista's exercise in pain reminded me of Nora Jean's. She had purposely gotten Mrs. Loughmiller mad at her. Why? Pain was the certain result. No, they didn't beat her with a belt or anything. They just made her suffer. When Mr. Loughmiller had arrived home, he'd grilled the steaks, the food was good, the conversation a bit awkward, and I'd said goodnight.

I didn't hear from Nora Jean for the rest of the weekend, but at lunch on Monday, she told me she was grounded. In New York, we called it "restricted." Nora Jean couldn't come over to my house, and I couldn't visit her after school either. We would be two weeks into summer vacation before we could hang out again.

Paul re-entered the room. He flicked clean, wet hands in front of me, making sure drops of water hit my face. Mom positioned him near the foot of Krista's crib. The side rail was down, and Krista lay on her back. She wore the top half of her one-piece footie pajamas while her skinny legs remained bare. Even in June, the warm PJs were needed for the desert nights.

"Start with your left hand holding Krista's heel," Mom instructed.

He grabbed her heel with confidence.

"Gently!"

He relaxed his hold.

Satisfied, she continued. "Now, with the right

hand, place the flat of your palm against the bottom of Krista's foot."

He followed the simple direction, but first he tickled her foot. She jerked it away and giggled.

Mom sighed. "Paul, be serious. It's important to do this correctly."

"Okay, okay." He took hold of Krista's heel again and placed the palm of his hand against the sole of her foot.

"Right. That's how it should look when you start. No! Don't press yet!"

He let go. "Sheesh."

Mom gave him The Look, lips tightened to a thin line, eyes squinting. "Do you want to do this or not?"

He cleaned up the attitude, fast. "Yes. I want to do this."

"Then understand that pressing on her foot is the tricky part. You want it firm, but not so hard that the foot bends back too fast. That will really hurt, maybe even cause damage." He nodded and she continued. "Watch me do it."

She removed Krista's foot from his grasp, putting her hands in the same positions. Then she pressed the foot so it would flex. At the same time Mom slid her left hand along the back of Krista's leg until she reached the knee. She pushed on my sister's thigh so the knee would bend. Krista knew to do that part herself, but we kept a hand there as a guide.

Mom pressed a little more against the sole of Krista's foot, and her toes started to angle toward the ceiling. "See? The harder I press, the more her calf muscles stretch."

Krista's brows knit together as if she were going to

frown, but she giggled instead. After a moment, Mom eased the pressure. "That's her signal that it's starting to hurt." She kissed Krista's big toe, which brought another giggle. "I don't know why she laughs. If someone were hurting my leg, I'd try to kick them away."

She turned to Paul. "Ready? Gently."

"Yup." He took Mom's place by the crib. Heel in left hand, right palm against the sole of her foot. Press gently.

I could see he pushed too quickly. Krista screamed, and he dropped her foot as if he had burned his hand. Mom gathered her out of the bed, cuddling her with one arm and rubbing her leg with the other hand.

"I *did* press gently. As gently as I know how!" He ran out of the room.

Poor guy. He didn't know his own strength.

Krista calmed down quickly, and Mom settled her back on the crib mattress while she continued to massage the leg. "Okay? All better?"

Whether Krista could read her lips or not, who could tell, but she nodded her head as if she understood. Mom pointed to me. "Debbie's turn to do your exercises."

I moved into place. Krista frowned and pointed to Mom.

Mom pointed to herself. "Mommy do it?"

Krista nodded.

As I stepped aside to let Mom take my place, a memory flashed through my mind from two years ago when Mom was pregnant. I'd had all these great plans about what I would get to do with my freckle-faced, blue-eyed little sister. Reading together, playing duets on the piano, jumping rope. Leg-stretching exercises sure never occurred to me.

None of those pipe dreams would ever happen. Krista had *brown* eyes, *no* freckles, and she could barely walk much less learn to jump rope. The piano would never have meaning for her, and I wondered how she was going to learn to read when she couldn't even understand what people said.

Most of the time, I didn't let Krista's deafness and cerebral palsy bother me. We had fun together doing stuff like walking around the yard and teaching her words even if she couldn't say them. Even leg exercises were fun. But tonight, a tinge of sadness hung in the air like a barely-remembered nightmare. I guess with Paul so upset over the exercise mess-up tonight and Nora Jean's punishment, I got to feeling down, too.

Krista's legs were gaining strength, so we went on longer walks. We even explored the desert. My fears had faded, a little, and I actually admired the wild beauty surrounding me. We never traveled far. How much endurance did *any* two-year-old have? But we always noticed something new. A lizard sunning itself on a rock, a single bloom on a little cactus plant.

It sure was dusty though. We'd lived here for two months, and I'd never seen a cloud.

Early in June, as Krista and I explored the front yard, the sunlight suddenly dimmed. A huge, black cloud appeared overhead. With one shaft of lightning and a simultaneous crack of thunder, rain fell out of the sky like God had upended a barrel and dumped it. Too late, Krista and I scurried for the cover of the open garage, our clothes already soaked through.

So, this was a cloudburst.

The torrent drummed a pounding rhythm on the roof. Curtains of water pummeled the pavement then ran in small rivers washing away the dust. I stepped out of the garage, arms outstretched and face lifted toward the heavens, allowing beautiful, life-giving rain to drench every pore of my body. With hair plastered to my head and shorts and shirt clinging to me, I whirled around the driveway. My personal rain dance. Krista grinned and did her own dance inside the garage.

I swooped down on her, swung her into my arms, and waltzed back outside. We twirled in circles and more circles. Krista laughed so hard she got the hiccups, and I plopped us down on the driveway before I got too dizzy. The neighbors probably thought we were crazy. So what? They never talked to us anyway.

Lying on my back with a thousand needles of rain tattooing every inch of me, I felt close to Jesus, kind of like when I walked along the shoreline back home. With one huge wave, the ocean could crush me. Here, the desert held all kinds of dangers. One wrong step and I could die. But for this moment, I remembered God was bigger than the ocean or the desert, and my puny little self was safe.

"Debbie, get out of the rain this instant!" Mom stood in the garage, holding a dripping Krista who must have toddled back to a dry place.

I sat up and grinned at her. "Isn't it fantastic?"

"We'll see how fantastic you think it is while you're wiping dry your sister's braces. I certainly hope you haven't ruined them."

Oh, man. I hadn't even thought about that. If I had to replace those, I wouldn't see my allowance all the way through high school.

Chapter 14:
Little Legs in Trouble

I work like Ma-mi.
Swish, swish. Clean my pants. Good girl.
Why is Ma-mi mad?

Engrossed in the silent depths of *20,000 Leagues Under the Sea*, the sound of sloshing water on earth's surface transported me from book world to my bedroom. I headed for the bathroom to investigate.

Water poured over the edge of the sink, onto Krista's little stepstool, and continued to the floor. Who had put the rubber stopper in the drain? Who had turned on the faucets? This had Wade's fingerprints all over it. Krista would have had to climb onto the counter in order to reach them.

From the doorway, I stretched toward the sink. With two quick turns of the faucet handles and one yank on the plug's chain, the waterfall ceased to exist.

However, the sloshing came from the toilet. A naked Krista was busy. She dipped her training pants into the bowl, stirred them round and round, and then she held them up for inspection. Like Mom did. Although Mom made sure they didn't drip over the toilet seat and floor. Not satisfied, Krista repeated the process.

"Mom, you gotta come see this," I called down the hallway. "Krista is really getting the idea about potty training."

Accidents had happened a lot, especially if she was outside. Krista couldn't *say* she needed to go potty, so we watched for a telltale look on her face and then picked her up and ran for it. A skinny, almost two-year-old kid with leg braces was awfully heavy when you're racing from the front yard to the bathroom at the back of the house. We were usually too late.

I turned back to the bathroom just in time to see Krista drop her pants in the toilet and pull the flush handle.

"Oh, no! Wait!" I lunged for the pants, but it was too late. They were gone.

Mom's flipflops slapped the linoleum floor as she approached. "She's getting the idea? Did she sit herself down on the commode?"

She didn't wait for an answer once she saw water all over everything. "What happened? What do you mean she gets it? Is this urine all over the floor? And where are her braces?"

Krista's latest trick. She could undo the straps on those braces in less time than Houdini could escape handcuffs.

I couldn't answer for the braces, which had survived the cloudburst just fine, but I knew the "what happened" part. "I think it's mostly water. She was washing out her training pants."

Mom's eyes darted from the sink to the tub. "Where did she put them?"

I tried to stifle a giggle and failed. "Down the toilet."

"Down the toilet? That will ruin the plumbing. Why didn't you stop her?"

With each sentence her voice rose. The boys joined her at the door.

"What did she do?" Paul demanded. Mr. I'm-in-charge-when-Dad's-not-home.

Wade peered over Paul's shoulder.

"Did you put the plug in the drain?" I demanded.

Wade seemed genuinely shocked. "You think I helped her flood the bathroom?"

Appearing shocked didn't mean he really was. "I don't know. Did you?"

"No. I'm not stupid."

He had a point. Wade never tried to get in trouble on purpose.

Krista watched us, wearing nothing but a proud grin on her face, ready to take a bow for a brilliant performance.

Mom grabbed a towel and started mopping water.

"But what *happened?*" Paul repeated himself, sounding more self-important than the first time.

I filled him in. "Krista flushed her underpants down the toilet."

Wade's guffaw was instantaneous. Paul, however, took time to decide if he would continue the father role or play the brother. *Brother* won the coin toss, and he joined Wade in the *ha-ha* of bathroom humor. Krista's grin widened. Her brothers approved. She ignored Mom's frown.

A few days later, she repeated her new skills. Just like Mom, she swished the pants in the toilet. Unlike Mom, she failed to remove the underpants from the bowl before pulling the handle.

Mom ran for the bathroom when she heard the flush, and boy, was she mad this time. She spanked Krista and fumed around the house for the next hour.

I paced two steps behind her. "It's not like Krista was trying to break the toilet. She only wanted to help."

"Well, now she knows she is *not* helping." The kitchen became lemon fresh as Mom scrubbed the counter with a soapy sponge, her whole body leaning into the job. Daddy should have her wax the car. She'd leave it so polished she could use the hood as a make-up mirror.

Almost as tall as Mom, I looked straight into her eyes. "I don't think she knows why you're mad. Or what she did wrong. You're not being fair."

"She could have plugged up the toilet."

"She doesn't *know* that." Now *I* was getting irritated. "Besides, it didn't happen."

"Fine. When she does plug it up, we can rent a Port-a-Potty. See how you like that."

I stared at her. What could I say to such an absurd statement?

"What?" she demanded.

"You're getting too mad over something little. If the toilet overflowed, Krista would find out why she can't flush her pants. And if we couldn't fix it with a plunger, we'd call a plumber."

"Pretty expensive lesson."

"Yeah, but in twenty years, will you look back on it as one of the worst things that ever happened to you?"

Mom rolled her eyes. She shook her head. Her lips almost turned up in a smile. The sponge circled the counter with less force.

"You sound like your father." She enveloped me in a swift hug.

Wade crashed open the front door. "The ice cream truck is coming. Can we buy some?"

Mom's answer was almost always, "no," but she surprised him. "Wave him down. I'll be right out."

With a whoop, he tore back outside.

Mom handed me a dollar. "That should cover it. Let Krista have whatever she wants."

Once summer vacation started, we found out the temperature topped one hundred degrees every day. Too many hours outside, and we felt as limp as the petunias in the front yard. They keeled over every afternoon until someone poured more water over them. We also doused water on ourselves every day. Usually, at the base pool.

After a hot, dry, dusty morning, nothing was more refreshing than passing through the gate into the exuberant atmosphere of chlorine. And that first cool plunge reminded me of the cartoon character with his pants on fire who sits in a bucket of water with steam rising around him.

By late afternoon, the water reached bath temperature but still remained cooler than the air. A flotilla of pool toys guided by their owners in colorful bathing suits bobbed from one side of the shallow end to the other. Older kids, anywhere from ten years old to high school competed for the biggest cannonball splash, welcomed by all who sat near the pool's edge. Of course, Wade and Paul joined them.

Mothers filled every lounge chair on the pool's perimeter. Several beach towels hung from tables and chairs like a colorful and crazy art display while others were spread out on the concrete behind the moms.

I never spent time on the concrete. Heated by the sun, it could burn right through the towel. To get from our umbrella table to the pool, I hopped onto every wet spot I could reach to save my bare feet. If I left the pool at all, I joined Krista in the baby pool, at which point I could don my sunglasses and finally gain relief from the glare reflected on water and poolside alike.

I would've joined a group of girls who grabbed their tans next to the fence, but that wasn't as easy for me as joining the cannonball competition was for my brothers. A girl had to be invited to the fence, and nobody invited me. They lived on base, and since we didn't go to the same school, they didn't know me.

I was okay with the isolation. Nora Jean came with me sometimes. Besides, in six weeks, I'd be on the beach with my friends.

That thought stabbed at my conscience. I'd frolic on a beach with an ocean breeze, while Nora Jean ironed shirts in a house where the window box air conditioner couldn't keep up with the desert heat. I'd dip my toes in the cool North Atlantic while my father sweated in a Philippine jungle for his last leg of training. Survival training.

The big pool terrified Krista. Too much splashing, too many people, and the water was over her head. The kiddy pool was a different story. Free from the awkward braces, Krista scampered with her lopsided, tippy-toe gait around the edge of the pool. She spent entire afternoons pouring water from a pail to a bowl to a cup to the pool. When the pail was empty, we filled it up again, and she started over. She kicked and paddled across her private ocean as easily as any normal toddler.

Then she got careless. As she readied herself for a leap from the pool's edge, Krista slipped. Before her head went under the water, her chin crashed into the concrete lip of the pool.

Mom plucked her out, and blood poured down Krista's neck, staining her suit and continuing the length of her leg. "Debbie! Quick. Grab a towel."

I ran for our table as Krista's screams followed me. By the time I returned with two towels, the lifeguard had already provided one, and several women hovered around them offering advice.

"Yeah, she's gonna need stitches."

"You better get her over to the clinic."

"Let me take a look. I'm a nurse."

Mom removed the towel, and the nurse peeked at the wound which immediately sent new rivulets streaming. "Yes, that will take a few stitches."

Stitches? I'd never had stitches in my life. Poor Krista wasn't even two yet and needed them already.

Mom looked calm in the midst of all that blood. I was ready to throw up.

Come to think of it, Mom usually stayed calm in kid emergencies. She hadn't gotten upset when Wade stepped on a needle, and it slid into his foot so deep he needed surgery. She'd even held it together when he tried to do flips from the shower rod at bath time. Landing on the pointy faucet handle, he gouged his thigh so deeply the fat was hanging from the wound. Daddy scooped him up, Mom wrapped him in towels, and they sped to the ER.

After the hysterical emergency run for a spider *non*-bite, Mom probably didn't want a return trip to the clinic, but she nodded matter-of-factly and turned to the lifeguard, a gorgeous guy with a golden tan, sun-bleached hair, and dark sunglasses. "Will it be okay to leave my older children here? They're all good swimmers, but Debbie's not sixteen yet."

Meaning we'd be breaking pool rules for unaccompanied minors.

He looked me over, lifted his shades, and winked at me. "Close enough."

Mom opened her mouth.

Please don't scold him for flirting with a thirteen-year-old. Please don't.

She pursed her lips, raised one eyebrow, and gave me the "Watch yourself" look as we returned to our table. Handing Krista over to me, she said, "Keep up the pressure."

I pressed the towel against Krista's chin. She'd stopped crying, but her little body trembled against me. Mom slipped on her beach robe and picked up her purse. She reached for Krista, and we made the exchange, both of us careful not to drop the towel.

"Watch your brothers." She nodded toward the

lifeguard. "Not Mr. Sunshine. Okay?"

I rolled my eyes. "Like he's going to notice me."

A flock of tanned teenaged girls in skimpy bikinis surrounded him. My hip-hugger two-piece suit, and my peeling, sunburnt nose were no competition.

Chapter 15:
Goodbye to the Desert California

Mah-mi cleans the house.
Almost all my toys are gone.
That means we will move.

But I told Nora Jean I'd be there by ten."

My argument didn't make a dent in Mom's attitude.

"So, you'll be ten minutes late. Get to it, and you might even get there on time."

The storm building inside of me seemed awfully close to what Krista probably felt just before she exploded in a tantrum. Beyond my normal sulk, I could feel my jaw tighten and my eyes tense. "Just because the dishwasher broke doesn't mean I'm the only one who can wash up after breakfast. Get one of the boys to do it." I pivoted and headed for the front door.

"Deborah Lynn, get back here this instant."

I ignored the command.

"Debbie!"

The door slammed behind me, and I broke into a run. All the way down the hill.

What was my *problem?* I continued with a furious walk, breathless, and brushing away angry tears. Being the oldest was my problem. Being a girl. Being responsible. Being *nice.*

And that wasn't all. Waiting for the end of the week so *I* could help clean the house before we moved. So *I* could help pack up what we would take back with us. So *I* could help take care of Krista when I wasn't helping with the cleaning and packing. All of the above so I could live in a brand-new house and leave my father behind.

Nora Jean took one look at my face, pulled me through the living room and out onto the back patio before Mrs. Loughmiller could look up from her magazine. "I'm gonna show Debbie your newest lawn ornament," she said sliding shut the door.

To keep up the charade, she led me to the middle of the yard where a glass globe of pink and purple swirls sat on a cone-like cradle. Even though it was only mid-morning, her bare feet had to be burning on the sand.

"What's the matter?" she demanded in a whisper.

"My mother. Do this, Debbie. Do that, Debbie. Help me with this. Help me with that. I am so sick of her!" If only I could punch somebody.

Nora Jean frowned. "Is that all?" She made for the hammock at a Cat-on-a-Hot-Tin-Roof pace.

"Whaddya mean 'Is that all?' I'm like a slave in—" Comprehension hit me at the same moment my out-flung arm hit the globe, knocking it off its perch.

Our eyes met. Me: shock. Nora Jean: outrage. Both of us: fear.

"I'm sorry!" I ran to where the globe had rolled. At

least, it hadn't shattered.

Nora Jean followed me, ignoring the heat on her bare feet. Together, we examined the glass ball. An obvious crack followed a path a quarter of the way around. A small hole creating a perfect circle about the width of my thumb revealed its hollow center. Like a pink and purple bowling ball. I pictured myself holding the ball, thumb in the hole, and rolling it toward the collection of cactus plants set in formation by the back fence. Trying to stifle a snicker, I choked out a second apology.

"This thing cost thirty bucks," Nora Jean hissed. "And you're laughing? What is wrong with you?"

"I'm sorry." Third time I said that. "I get like this sometimes when I'm in really big trouble." I clapped my hand over my mouth in a vain effort to smother my absolutely inappropriate giggles.

Nora Jean glared at me. "*I'm* in really big trouble."

"But I was the one that hit it off the stand."

"She won't believe that. She'll think you're trying to keep *me* out of trouble."

My hysteria subsided. "You can't take the fall for this."

Nora Jean set the globe back on the cone like a mother laying a newborn infant in its crib, making sure the hole faced away from the house. The ball didn't crack any further. "Even if she believed you, she'd hit up your parents for fifty bucks."

"But you said it cost thirty."

She just stared at me, head cocked to the side with a "Don't you know anything?" look on her face.

"Still. They'd pay her. And you wouldn't get into trouble."

She grabbed my shoulder and brought her face real close to mine. "They always find something to punish me for, whether I did it or not. What's one more thing?" She heaved a sigh. "Never mind. It doesn't matter."

It did matter. *I* knew who should be punished.

Her fingers dug into me. "Look, I've been watching you for the last week. You're starting to fall apart. You gotta move again. I know what that's like. "They're taking you away from your dad. I've been there. They took me away from my brother."

"I'm sor—"

"Don't you say that again!" She shook me.

"I meant being sorry about what I said just as I hit that pink and purple bowling ball."

She stepped back and glanced at the globe, then at me. And nearly bust a gut laughing. "It does look like a bowling ball. No wonder you lost it."

"But I wasn't even thinking about you. You've got it far worse than me. Washing a few extra dishes? I can't believe I was complaining about dishes to *you*."

She sobered. "Don't worry about me."

"I wish I could take you with us."

"I wish—" she shook her head and gazed at a lone hawk circling far above us. When it was lost to sight, she returned her attention to me. "I don't wish anything. If I want something, I make it happen." She put on that careless smile. "So don't worry about me."

Mom had washed all of our clothes, and we were on strict orders not to get dirty for the next two days. She had a laundry bag reserved for today's underwear that would be stowed in a separate compartment of her luggage. I tried not to think about *those* details.

Tomorrow, we would board the plane for home. My *real* home. I didn't want to think about the details of that either. My feelings pulled every which way.

My friends in New York. Yay!

Saying goodbye to Nora Jean. Boo.

Saying goodbye to the desert. Yay! No, boo. I'd grown to admire its rugged beauty. Exploring the Mojave on Harvey's scooter had given me the opportunity to get to know it without fear, just a healthy respect, like I respected the ocean's magnificent power.

I'd kind of miss Harvey, too. Boo.

Living near the ocean again. Yay!

No purple mountain majesty. Boo.

Seeing Chip again. Yay!

Not seeing Bryce anymore. Boo. Sort of. The other girls in youth group told me Bryce dated around at his high school. So what? By my second Sunday, I had figured out he was as smooth as pudding, but there wasn't much flavor to his artificial vanilla. I'd had fun being his girlfriend at church, enjoying his entertaining stories—all of them about himself. No, my heart belonged to Chip. Even if he did write only two letters in four months.

Saying goodbye to Daddy. *Boo.* For the last week, I couldn't even escape into a book. It seemed every story had families forced apart for one reason or another. *Gone With the Wind*. War. Don't want to think about it. *Exodus*. The Holocaust. Even worse than war. *A Wrinkle in Time*. Galactic separations. *Cheaper by the Dozen*. In real life, the dad had died.

Mom interrupted my desperate attempt to get

interested in a teen fan magazine. "Here." She handed me the dust mop. "Pull your bed from the wall and mop every corner of this room including the closet."

After slamming out of the house that day, I'd been given plenty of hard labor. At least all the work kept dark thoughts at bay. Sometimes.

With a sigh, I dropped my copy of *Teen Magazine* onto my bed. Start with the closet. It held the shoes I'd be wearing tomorrow and my travel outfit. Three times back and forth on the two-by-four-foot space, and a couple of dust bunnies tumbled into the room. I swabbed under the bed, pulled it away from the wall as instructed, and slid the mop along the baseboards. I amassed a miniscule blond-brown hairball, an ant, and a peanut shell. How long had *that* been there? I don't eat peanuts.

I even pulled the dresser from its wall and mopped away. Lots of dust and—what? A dead scorpion? Don't panic. Remember. It's *dead*.

And my brothers said I was crazy for praying for protection every night. *Thank You, thank You, thank You, God.*

The doorbell rang while I was sweeping the small pile into a dustpan.

Nora Jean appeared in my doorway. "Hey," she said.

"Hey," I responded. "I thought I was supposed to go to your place in about an hour."

She grinned. "They gave me the day off just for you."

Sure enough, Mr. Loughmiller had discovered the damaged "bowling ball" within twenty-four hours. Nora Jean had been on lockdown ever since, but Mrs.

Loughmiller had allowed for one last visit. I was still an angel in her mind.

"Can you have lunch with us? We're eating the last of the salami and peanut butter and jelly in the house."

"Okay. I should go back by four so I can get dinner ready, though."

Of course.

It was too hot to stay outside for long. One hundred and ten degrees, even in desert heat, can only be tolerated for a few minutes without getting "dirty." We took Krista for a walk in her stroller, then ambled into the desert for "one last look" before I left. Harvey joined us.

"Maybe you and Nora Jean can go out on your scooter after I leave," I said.

She offered him a sardonic smile, and Harvey turned a dusky shade of pink.

When the heat drove us inside, Nora Jean and I watched soap operas. Boring. But I knew she didn't want to go home, and I didn't want to say goodbye.

At 3:45, I left Nora Jean to *Dark Shadows* and went back to my room. I opened the dresser's top drawer and removed a small box decorated with seashells, the only item left in the drawer. This would be goodbye.

When I returned to the living room, Nora Jean was rummaging in the backpack she had brought with her. She pulled out a neatly wrapped box and flourished it in front of her. "I brought you a good luck gift."

I held up the box. "I have something for you, too. But I didn't think about wrapping it."

"You have a gift? For me?"

The delight on her face just about did me in.

Hadn't the Loughmillers ever given her a gift?

I handed over the box and received her package. She lifted the lid and looked at me, a question on her face.

"Remember the day Krista said 'Ow?' That was the day you showed her two rocks. One sharp and jagged. The other smooth."

Nora Jean nodded.

"I know I'm going to be a teacher someday," I said. "You're a born teacher, too, Nora Jean."

She lifted the contents of the box into her hand. One jagged rock. One smooth.

"You automatically knew how to teach Krista the idea of rough and smooth, so I thought I'd use rocks like that to remind you that you *can* be one of the best teachers ever."

I couldn't tell her the stones had a second meaning. Nora Jean would assume I pitied her. She'd endured so many hurts. Jagged rocks had been thrown at her for fifteen years. The rough granite in the box signified her past. The polished pink quartz represented the smooth, beautiful life I wanted for her.

Still, she said nothing. Had I insulted her with a gift of rocks?

"I guess I could've spent money on some little doodad that didn't mean much to either one of us, but I hoped you'd understand what the rocks meant. Kind of a symbol."

Eyes glistening, for Nora Jean would never let *anyone* see her cry, she said, "I get it. Thanks. Open yours."

"Cool wrapping paper." I peeled the psychedelic design off of the flat box she had given me.

Inside the box, lay a necklace of turquoise and sea green hippie beads, the only gift her older brother had ever given to her.

"Oh, Nora Jean."

She might have been able to hold back tears, but I was lost. "I can't take these to New York. Far away from you."

"Yes, you can. The colors remind me of the sea which made me think of you. As soon as I'm out of school next year, I'll be living with Kase, so I won't miss them for long. When you wear these beads, think of me."

I flung my arms around her. "I will *never* forget you."

Chapter 16:
Going Home

We go up, up, up.
Da-di does not go with us.
I wonder how long…

I still hated California, but I would've stayed forever if it meant Daddy wouldn't go to Vietnam.

We crammed ourselves and our luggage into the Renault once again and drove back through the mountains to the airport in Los Angeles. It was like the opening scene of one of those predictable movies as the family waves goodbye when Father goes off to war. Except *Father* waved goodbye to the *family,* and I didn't know how the story would end.

War stories from Hollywood look so romantic. The Flying Tiger darting through wisps of flak. The hero belly-landing his wounded plane, the lone survivor of his squadron. Those with minor roles perish in plumes of black smoke. The hero's beautiful wife runs to greet him upon arriving home. Passionate kiss. Happily ever after.

War in real life? Fear lurks under the surface like a

hungry crocodile.

If cameras were rolling as we said goodbye to Daddy, they would focus on our family as crowds of extras streamed past. They would zoom in as I leaned into Daddy's arms one last time, inhaling his after shave one last time, squeezing him tight one last time. Microphones would catch his murmur in my ear. "Help your mother in any way she asks."

The camera would zoom even closer on my fingers as I promised, cross my heart and hope to die.

Krista studied our faces while we held onto Daddy with such extra intensity. He was often away for days at a time, so she probably wondered why we looked so sad. Why did Daddy have to peel Wade off his chest and hand him over to Mom?

How could any toddler understand the idea of living for an entire year without her daddy?

Still, in the movie of my mind, I watched us walk out on the tarmac, heat rising in visible waves. We march up the steps to the plane. The stoic mother, chin up, head high, refusing to cry. The eldest daughter holding back the tears, too. The brothers. Solemn. Dry-eyed.

Was my dad the star in this movie, or did he only have a bit part? He was the hero to *me*. I thought back to Shirley Temple in *The Little Princess*. Sara Crewe had found her Dad alive. *My* dad *had* to be the one who escaped anti-aircraft fire. He *had* to land his jet safely. Mom needed him. Krista needed him. We all needed him. God would make sure he'd come back.

Paul, Wade, and I sat in one row of seats. Mom and Krista were in the row behind us. Paul, as the oldest son, had once again put on the solemn mantle of "man of the house."

The plane lifted off spearing its way eastward over the desert. I stared at the brown and gray landscape below. Somewhere down there lay Masterville. That's when the tears erupted.

Poor Nora Jean. She'd known from the day we met that I wouldn't be staying. She stuck with me anyway. I'd given her my new address, but I would never receive a letter. Writing was too much like school, and school just wasn't Nora Jean's thing. Would she escape the Loughmillers? And if she succeeded, would she have a good job some day? A nice husband? Would she be a mom? I'd never know.

Once the plane leveled off at top altitude, the land below looked like a physical map with only ripples for mountains and all the desert colors melting into a dull tan. I fled into a mystery novel until we landed.

Chicago was *green*. Trees. Grass. If I'd been outside, I would've kissed the ground, but we were only staying for an hour before the same plane took off again for LaGuardia Airport. I'd get my chance though, once we were back in New York. The Fadlers would pick us up in our own car. They'd been keeping it for us so we didn't have to put it in storage. The plan was to spend the night at their home in the green, green countryside of St. James, then drive to Hampton Shores the next day. Five of us spread out in a giant station wagon. Luxury!

"Can we get off the plane?" Paul jogged in place, ready to run a marathon—anywhere. "We've been sitting for hours."

Mom regarded both boys, doubt in her eyes. "We'll all stretch our legs for a bit. But stay near the gate. No wandering all over the airport."

We trooped down the enclosed corridor. Mom stopped at the first row of seats once we set foot in the terminal. Gate 15H. The boys wove their way through the bustle of passengers to a store packed with magazines across the way.

Worry lines creased Mom's forehead. "Keep an eye on them, will you? The last thing I need is lost kids in this crowd."

I crossed to the store and discovered they sold books as well as magazines. The boys were engrossed in Superman comics, so I checked out the bestsellers. Mom had given up on limiting me to kids' books. I preferred historical novels, especially stories from World War II.

The buzz of the crowds and the garbled voices from the intercom faded as I breathed in the glorious perfume of fresh ink on pristine paper and studied the jackets of several titles. Ah! *Up the Down Staircase,* a story about a teacher, kind of like the movie *To Sir, With Love*. I thumbed through the pages. Just a bunch of letters and memos. I wasn't spending my allowance money on that.

Mom appeared at my side with Krista on her hip. "Where are your brothers?"

"Looking at comic books."

"No. They're not. They're not here. You were supposed to be watching them."

She trusted me in a *book*store? My gaze scanned the two little aisles. No Paul. No Wade. My heart began an accelerated lub-dub. "They were here a minute ago."

Mom's sigh was as sharp as a new razor blade. "Keep Krista with you. I'm going to look for them." She thrust Krista into my arms and skirted past another customer. "Boarding call is in ten minutes," she called over her shoulder. "Get on the plane whether I come back with your brothers or not."

Neither Mom nor Paul and Wade returned. People lined up to board. The intercom squawked, urging passengers to get on the plane. With numb, wooden legs, I carried Krista down the corridor and found our seats. Stranger after stranger paraded past us thumping carry-on luggage into the overhead compartments. But no Mom, no brothers.

Finally, the boys ran toward me, full of smiles.

"Where's Mom?" I asked.

"I dunno." Wade hopped into the row in front of me.

"*We* haven't seen her." Paul rolled a candy wrapper into a ball and aimed for the ash tray in the arm of the window seat. Two points. "We got this out of a machine. Then we came back, and they showed us where the pilot sits. It was great!"

"Yeah, it was great," Wade echoed. "We got to sit in his seat and pretend to fly the plane. We're honorary pilots." He pointed to the tin wings pinned to his shirt.

"You mean you've been on the plane all this time? Oh, boy." I scanned the passengers inching down the aisle, burdened with luggage. No sign of our mother. "Mom's searching the airport for you."

"She'd better get back. It's almost time to take off." Paul peered down the aisle as if Mom were an irresponsible child. I wanted to smack the know-it-all look off his face.

Mom appeared in the doorway, chest heaving. Fear hadn't left her eyes by the time she reached our seats. "Where have you been?" she gasped. "I was ready to hold the plane until I could find you!"

"They were in the cockpit." If I had done my job, I would have known that in the first place.

"Why didn't you tell me?" She shot a searing look at the boys.

"We didn't know that you didn't know where we were." Paul put on his innocent look, although for once, he really was innocent.

"We thought you saw us," Wade added.

Mom sank into the seat, still breathless. "It's okay. We're all here now. Nobody's fault."

But it was *my* fault. Me and books. Maybe I needed to stop reading. Next time Mom asked me to help, I wouldn't open a book until the job got done. I had promised Daddy.

Chapter 17:
Move-In Day

Sticky orange squares.
Hiding game behind boxes.
The boys make me laugh.

Call me a veteran of moving days. I've packed and unpacked my stuff more times than Mary Poppins.

Ever since we were old enough to walk, the boys and I knew the unique fun of Move-In Day. Before the van arrived, we played in empty closets and clomp-clomped through hallways, our footsteps echoing on bare floors. As furniture filled the rooms, we played hide and seek. There were a zillion places to hide, especially since a new hiding place was created every time a carton was added to a room.

Once the moving men drove away, we peeled off the numbered stickers on furniture and stuck them on ourselves. A houseful of furniture left us well-decorated by the end of the day.

This would be Krista's first Move-In Day. Our relocation to California didn't count. The furnished rental in Masterville never required a moving van. This morning, we would enter an empty building, and we would go to bed in a house filled with a jumble of boxes piled around familiar furniture.

Since Daddy wasn't here to help, Mom took over Dad's job of directing the moving men. My expected assignment of watching Krista was passed on to the boys. Mom relegated her old job of the checklist to me. *Every* carton on the delivery list as well as *every* piece of furniture entering the house needed to be accounted for. I finally understood why *every* item had a sticker.

When we moved out of our old house four months earlier, workers had placed a numbered sticker on everything going into storage. They wrote the name of the item beside the matching number on the inventory list. The stickers identified everything we owned from the sleeper sofa to the towel boxes. By the time the van was empty, every sticker should be accounted for and every item on the list checked off.

I loved lists. I loved this job. And I was too old to play in closets.

With my handy-dandy clipboard and a fine-point pen, I watched item after item parade past me. Did the number on the list match the number on the item passing by? Check. Did the list's description of the furniture match the item passing by? Check. Next.

The thuds and bumps of the moving men with Mom's voice in the background added to the rhythm. Every once in a while, I heard a giggled shriek from Krista as Paul or Wade pounced on her hiding place during their all-day game of hide and seek.

I paused in my concentration to caress a smooth maple headboard. Tonight, I would sleep in my *own* bed for the first time in over four months. An ocean breeze would waft through my open windows. This might be a brand-new house, but I was already home.

We took an hour to go out for lunch, then got right back to work. Number, item, match, check, next. Paul's pup tent bundled in tape passed through. He grabbed it as soon as I checked it off and ran out the back door. After another hour of number, item, match, check, next, the parade stopped. I looked toward the street for more incoming, but the moving men were lifting the dollies into the van. I checked my list. Lines and lines of checkmarks, but—two empty spaces.

What was missing? #60811. Twin headboard. Oops. Petting the headboard had cost me a check mark. My pen filled in the empty space. #61109. Kitchen utensils. This would take some searching.

Kitchen first, in case I just forgot to check it off. I stared at twenty or more boxes on the floor, the counters, the table. Ten minutes later, no #61109.

I followed voices to the back of the house where Mom had the men putting together bed frames for her.

"Mom!"

I pointed to the empty space in my otherwise pristine list of checks on my clipboard. She nodded and turned toward the men.

"Excuse me. We're short one box of kitchen items."

"And I double-checked in the kitchen to make sure I didn't miss it when you came through," I added.

The young man grimaced like he didn't believe me, but the older guy moved toward the door. "I'll check the truck."

"Thank you." Mom smiled. "And we'll inspect

boxes in the other rooms in case it got misplaced."

I didn't see how I could have missed it on the checklist *and* the men put it in the wrong room. Once she led me out of the bedroom, I said as much.

"Stranger things have happened. And this way, the men know we're doing our part in case it was your mistake and not theirs." She tapped the clipboard. "You've actually done a better job than I ever did with a list of hundreds of items. Daddy and I usually have to comb through a ton of boxes looking for at least ten missed numbers."

Wow. The first household job I'd ever done better than my mom.

"Mrs. Hansen," a voice called from the vicinity of the kitchen.

We hurried through the dining room.

The older man patted a carton on the kitchen floor. "Found it tucked behind the mirror of our next delivery."

Good old #61109. With tremendous satisfaction I filled the gap in the column of checks. My job was done.

I handed the clipboard to Mom. "Sticker time?" I might be too old for hide and seek, but I couldn't stand the idea of missing the sticker search. She wouldn't make me unpack boxes right away, would she?

Mom hesitated, then laughed. "Go ahead."

I spun and ran to the foot of the stairs. "Paul. Wade. It's time!"

At first, Krista stared at us like we were crazy. Her big brothers and sister were peeling little orange squares off chairs, bed rails, and tables, and putting them on arms, legs, and faces.

Wade put one of his stickers on the back of Krista's hand. "See? It sticks. Fun!" he smiled at her.

Krista only looked confused. Wade guided Krista's hand to a sticker on a table leg. "You do it." He pointed at her.

Krista didn't move.

Again, he took her hand, and this time forced her finger to pull back the corner of the sticker. "Peel it off." He nodded his head toward the sticker.

Krista peeled it off.

"Yeah!"

"That's right!"

"You did it!"

"Now put it on yourself." Paul removed a sticker from his hand and placed it on the end of his nose.

Krista burst out laughing. She looked at her sticker, and then put it on *her* nose and grinned. We ran to the bathroom, and I picked her up so she could look in the mirror. A little girl clown with merry brown eyes and an orange sticker on her nose stared back at her.

After that lesson, Krista knew exactly what to do. By supper time, the four of us were covered with at least thirty stickers apiece. Paul, Wade, and I peeled ours off and stuck all of them on Krista. We nicknamed her "Sticker Child" and brought her to Mom, who was putting sheets on the beds.

She observed us with a smile. "Very funny."

We grinned with satisfaction and started to strip Krista of stickers and reattach them to ourselves.

Mom raised an eyebrow. "However, we're invited to the Whalens for dinner tonight. Are you going dressed in orange squares?"

"Yes," we chorused.

"No," she said. "Take them off, throw them away, and wash up before we go. I hung up towels in the bathroom."

We trudged down the hall.

Wade got a familiar gleam in his eye. "Let's each keep one sticker stuck on some place where Mom can't see."

"Okay." I loved the sneakiness.

"Good idea." Paul placed one of his stickers on his stomach under his shirt.

When we left the house, Wade's sticker was on his shoulder, mine on the back of my neck covered by long hair, and Krista's on the inside of her knee concealed by the leg brace. As she walked out the door beside Mom, she turned to look at me. She pointed to her knee, covered her mouth, and giggled. I held a finger to my lips in a "shh" motion.

Mom turned. "Are you making funny faces at her or something?"

"Something like that." I offered my most innocent smile.

Chapter 18:
Great Reunions

Nobody will play.
Boxes, boxes, and boxes.
I play by myself.

We unpacked all morning. Hot work. I'd gotten used to the air conditioning in California, but only the richest people had it back home. Although the ocean breeze usually kept everybody comfortable for miles inland, we'd moved in the middle of a heat wave. Mom promised if we got most of our work done, we could go to the beach in the afternoon.

The very last box in my room, hidden behind the others, must have arrived while Grandma moved in last week. It contained my purple and blue bedspreads and the matching curtains to go with the lavender walls and multi-hued rug. This was going to look great! When Grandma returned from Aunt Irma's, she was going to love my room.

By lunchtime, I had everything just the way I wanted it. I even got my brownie camera and took a few pictures.

We ate on the back deck, our only hope for a hint of air movement.

"Can I ride my bike to Chip's? I know how to get there." I swallowed my last bite of a bologna sandwich.

"I thought you wanted the beach," Mom said.

"But we won't go until after Krista's nap, right?"

Mom nodded. "Make sure you're back by two."

Chip's house was on the other side of the village, but in such a small town, it was hard to get lost. Boy, would he be surprised. He'd written me in June about his summer camp plans for late August, so he should be home. Last week, I sent a letter telling him when I'd be back. I included my new phone number and warned him it might take a few days of settling in before I'd have time to see him. But here I was, heading his way, on my second day in Hampton Shores.

I pedaled down the driveway wearing a new hot pink tee shirt and my favorite jeans shorts. The Great Reunion. Only ten minutes away. Would he hug me? Hold my hand? *Kiss* me? I'd let Bryce kiss me back in California. It was kind of sloppy. Chip could probably kiss better. If not, I didn't see what was so great about kissing a guy.

When I reached Main Street, the crowd distracted me from daydreams. Although we had driven through town on many Sundays in the summer, Hampton Shores appeared a bit different at bicycle level. From the car, we'd always laughed at the tourists parading up and down the sidewalks, many of them dressed in ridiculous outfits.

This time, I was part of the crowd as I tried to cross a busy intersection. And it wasn't even the weekend yet. A guy with long, uncombed brown hair and a bushy beard to match sauntered by with his girlfriend, whose braided brown hair reached past her waist. Raggedy Ann and Raggedy Andy Hippie Twins. Both wore tattered, flowered, bell-bottomed pants. She sported a white tee-shirt with the sleeves torn off. He had a string of purple beads around his neck, no shirt.

From the opposite direction, a skinny old lady in a lime-green miniskirt minced down the sidewalk. She wore a matching, sleeveless sequined top and high-heeled sandals with pink rhinestones. The bulging blue veins running up and down her legs did *not* go with the rest of the outfit.

Dashing across the street during a lull in the traffic, I almost ran my bike into an exquisitely dressed couple in white. I would've died if my tire had put a mark on those immaculate slacks.

My first thought: "I almost bumped into Sonny and Cher." Both were elegant, darkly tanned, with several gold chains around their necks, just like the famous singing duo. The bracelets, rings, and earrings had to weigh them down on such a hot day. The guy wore as much make-up as the lady, and it was melting along the edge of his receding hairline.

"Excuse me," I mumbled. They stared at me, then moved slightly to one side, royalty of the Hamptons deigning to let me pass.

Two blocks to go. I passed stores with colorful awnings, several with piped music coming through their open doors. The aroma of grilled burgers beckoned visitors to enter Valeria's Bistro. Turning right, I wheeled past the quaint town library and beautiful, old-money homes with perfect lawns and hedges. My legs pumped faster, and then—Tidal Drive. Only a block from the bay.

I braked when I reached Chip's mailbox, breathing in the humidity and feasting my eyes on the old, familiar scrub pines across the road. No more dry heat and desert wasteland. Salt air containing a hint of pine drifted past my nose, and a moist breeze caressed my arms and face. Instead of buzzards, gulls flew overhead diving from my view to pluck a fish from the sea, then soaring up again with the prize.

I pedaled up the long driveway to Chip's house, tall and stately and painted gray. I'd forgotten Chip's family was wealthy. Flowering shrubs created a fringe beneath the windows. Giant oaks grew close to the house leaving it shaded and cool. A single bird called, and I was aware of the thrum of the ocean.

I parked the bike, walked up the flagstone path bordered with coral roses in full bloom, and rang the doorbell. No one answered. As my finger aimed to press the button again, the door opened, and a pale lady, unsmiling, stared at me through the screen. She reminded me of Miss Clavel from the Madeline books.

"Yes?"

"Hi, I'm Debbie Hansen. Is Chip here?" Maybe her stiff manner was just my imagination. "I've been in California for four months, and we got back this week. I wrote and said I'd try to see him."

"He is not home right now."

"Oh." I dazzled her with my brightest smile. "Please tell him I came by, and he can call me."

Her face showed no expression, but I felt like a bug under a microscope. "I will tell him you were here."

That didn't sound promising. Guess I didn't know

how to dazzle after all. Walking down the path, I remembered my manners. "Thank you. Good-bye."

She closed the door. Miss Clavel was nicer.

So much for the Great Reunion. And that woman probably wouldn't tell him anything.

I shook off the bad vibes. I'd lived that way for four months and wasn't going to do the same now that I was home.

There were still plenty of things to do today. I had a little money with me so I could buy a flower for Grandma's room before I biked back. Kind of a welcome home gift. I couldn't wait to get to the Air Force beach again. Maybe some of my old friends would be there, although most of their dads had been reassigned by now.

And I could add extra touches to my *lavender* room—mine and Krista's—when we got back from the beach. It was fun last night, to share a room again. No problems getting Krista to go to bed in *this* new house.

At the end of the path, I stooped to take in the scent of one rose and gazed back at the house. If the regal lady was watching, she probably didn't want my common nose near her precious flowers. I dared to run my finger over its waxy petals, then plucked one and slipped it in my pocket.

As long as I was running around town, I decided to bicycle over to Cathy Morris's house, and we could figure out how to get my goldfish back home. I totally forgot about them yesterday.

Cathy lived on the opposite side of town from Chip, so it took a few minutes to reach her modest little neighborhood near the elementary school. Happy memories of friends and sixth grade wafted over me like a gentle breeze as I passed the building. If I turned right, I'd get to the junior-senior high school where I would start eighth grade in a month and be back with old friends. People I could count on instead of the stand-offish kids in California.

I rolled to a stop in Cathy's driveway and hopped off the bike. The door opened before I knocked, and Cathy's redheaded younger sister, Natalie, greeted me with a cunning smile and chilling words. "Hi, Debbie. If you're looking for Cathy the Terrible, she went into hiding."

"Why is she terrible, and why is she hiding?" Although I had an awful feeling I knew the answer.

Natalie opened the door, holding on to that nasty smile. "I'll make her come out of hiding to tell you."

As I slipped inside, she bellowed toward the back of the little house. "Cathy! Debbie's here to see you!"

Silence. We waited. Maybe for two whole minutes. I stared at the threadbare sofa. A corner of the sand-colored rug had unraveled. Mrs. Morris peeked her head into the room from the kitchen. "No Cathy? I'll go get her. Sorry about that, Debbie."

Sorry that Cathy hadn't shown her face, or sorry about my fish?

Natalie followed her mom, but no one invited me further into the house.

Another two minutes, and I heard feet scuffling on the kitchen floor. Natalie bobbed around the corner, eyes gleaming with anticipation for the scene about to unfold. Cathy appeared behind her holding the goldfish bowl—my heart lifted in hope—but no, the bowl was empty.

When she was about two feet away, Cathy finally

looked up from the floor. "I'm sorry, Debbie. I did everything you told me to do. I guess the change was just too much for them."

"It's okay. They were getting old." I didn't want her feeling guilty. "It's really my fault for making them move to a different house." So now I felt guilty instead. "You know how people get cranky and don't want anything to change when they're old? I guess it's the same for fish."

Cathy held out the bowl to me, but I shook my head. "You keep it. Or throw it away. I can't carry it on my bike, and I don't plan to put any new fish in it."

Cathy nodded and clutched the bowl to her chest. Nobody talked. Not even Natalie, but she stared daggers at her sister.

I was ready to get out of there. "See you at church, okay?"

"Yeah, see you at church."

I let myself out, but as I straddled my bike, Natalie raced out the door at full steam.

She grabbed the handlebars and hissed my name. "She *lied* to you. The fish *weren't* too old. She forgot to feed them after the first *week*."

I blinked at her intensity.

She seemed to take that as a sign that I didn't believe her. "Really. Mom asked her four days in a row if she had fed the fish. And on the fifth day they were dead."

Cathy didn't feed them? Poor George and Marty starved to death? Pictures of my poor babies swimming in slower and slower circles until they floated on the surface, lifeless, filled my mind. I took a deep, shaky breath. "Thanks for telling me, Nat." Her revelation had rolled the weight of guilt off of my shoulders like a thousand-pound dumbbell.

She reared back as if I had hit her. "Cathy killed your fish, and you're not mad?"

"I feel bad that Cathy ended up the wrong person to take care of them. But at least I tried to keep them alive."

Natalie didn't look convinced.

"You know where my dad is right now, don't you?" I figured everybody in town did.

"He had to go fight in a war," she said.

"So, when I think about my fish, and then I think about my dad… Can you see why I might not be mad?"

The fire left her eyes and she nodded. "Fish aren't people."

Natalie was a smart little cookie.

Chapter 19:
The Duck Pond

Deh-bee calls them duhs.
I was afraid. Would they bite?
They ate bread instead.

Grandma arrived at exactly eleven o'clock the next morning, pressing us to her in a cloud of Chanel No. 5 perfume and Coty face powder. She handed each kid a Lifesaver candy. Grandpa used to save butter rum flavor for me, but Grandma only had the fruit flavors so I picked pineapple. I missed butter rum. I missed Grandpa.

We rushed her upstairs where we'd decorated her new bedroom-sitting room. My single carnation stood in a slim bud vase. The boys had lined up their favorite Matchbox cars along the top of her bookcase, and Krista had donated one of her stuffed animals. The neon pink hippo lounged against a row of olive-green pillows resting on Grandma's combination divan/bed.

She set her carpetbag of a pocketbook on the floor next to her elegant little desk. "Isn't it lovely to move into a brand, new house?"

Glancing at my flower, she smiled, bent toward it, and offered a little sniff. She caressed the hippo with one finger while Krista hugged her leg.

Wade pointed to the cars. "We thought you might like stuff on the top. It was pretty bare."

He rolled the end car off the shelf, and Grandma winced. The wheels might scratch the wood. "Everything looks perfect," she pronounced.

Which I doubted. Grandma was the one who always looked perfect, her silvery hair arranged in a chignon with not one strand out of place. Her dresses never wrinkled, and pale pink polish always graced her manicured nails.

Grandma's room would look completely different in a week. Porcelain knickknacks would adorn the bookcase, and the pink hippo would find its way back to Krista's bed. But Grandma would figure out how to keep everyone's feelings from being hurt.

We dragged her through the rest of the house, and she complimented all of it, even though a carton or two still littered every room except the little bathroom off the kitchen. "Two and a half baths!" she exclaimed. "No line if you need the facilities." The den looked "wonderfully cozy," the kitchen was "roomy and well-equipped." The dining room had a "nice, formal touch to it," and the living room, "positively regal." She even praised the unfinished basement.

We arrived at Krista's and my room. "It's so feminine," Grandma said.

I wanted "feminine." With the colors I had chosen, the room had a cool, serene atmosphere. Even the large shag rug was lavender and blue with a little aqua mixed in, far more plush than Grandma's forest green tightly-woven carpet.

My room would be my haven. In the evenings, I could look out my west windows and watch the sun sink behind the trees in our wooded back yard. I'd feel peaceful all over. Kind of like how I felt when I watched the sun rise over "my mountain" back in the desert.

While Grandma unpacked, I took Krista for a long walk around the neighborhood in her stroller. A few of the neighbors introduced themselves. One lady across the street had two little kids. Maybe I could babysit for them.

Krista and I stopped at a pond. Actually, the pond was on our left, and a finger of the bay was on our right with enough land in between to hold a narrow road. The hot, still air held a bit of a stink, maybe a combination of the barely moving, brackish water and rotting plants in the marshy surroundings. Ducks paddled in the pond, and swans glided in lazy circles on the other side.

Krista's head swung left to the ducks, then right to the swans, then back again. She could tell these animals weren't pets, but they weren't caged either like in the zoos she'd visited. She climbed out of the stroller to get a better look at the ducks.

They rushed out of the water and flocked to her, quacking and flapping their wings. Surely, she had breadcrumbs for them. Krista screamed and tried to run, but the braces wouldn't allow her to move fast enough. She tripped, sprawling on the sand. I scooped her up and walked back to the stroller while she sobbed into my neck.

Without any visible food, the ducks lost interest and waddled back to the water.

"See?" I forced Krista's chin in the direction of the pond then back to face me. "See? No 'ow.' They won't hurt you."

I wiped the snot off her face, using the edge of her shirt. I made the sign for "eat" and pointed to the ducks. They wanted something to eat. Big mistake. She shrieked right into my ear and burst into new tears. She must've thought the ducks wanted to eat *her*.

Light bulb on! I rushed back home bumping the stroller over the asphalt at top speed. Motioning for Krista to wait, I darted into the house and grabbed two slices of bread. We returned to the duck pond, and I parked the stroller as close to the ducks as I dared without Krista screaming her head off.

"Watch." I placed my fingers on her cheeks directly under her eyes, then I pointed to myself.

I strolled to the edge of the pond, tore off a piece of bread, and threw it in the water. A duck dove for it. I looked back at Krista. She stared at the ducks with renewed interest.

"Come on," I waved to her.

She shook her head vigorously.

The ducks left the water and crowded closer to me. I tossed another piece of bread. Three ducks snapped at it. Two butted heads, and the third swallowed the prize.

I waved again.

She raised up her arms, asking me to help her out of the stroller. She wasn't about to walk up to those ducks all by herself.

I lifted her out, handed her the other slice of bread, and with my hand on her shoulder, I propelled her to the water's edge. Although still jumpy, she crumbled the bread like I did and threw it into the air. The ducks snagged every crumb. When the bread was gone, Krista stood relaxed and smiling as the flock swam to the middle of the pond.

In bed that night, I got to thinking how great it was to be *home*. To have my sister share my room again. She slept soundly in her "big girl" bed three feet away, making soft breathy noises. I could sniff the salt air, and I was surrounded by lush greens of trees and grass outside my window. In a few weeks, I'd be back at school with all my friends.

The only thought to disturb my peace? Chip hadn't called.

Chapter 20:
Desert in New York

Deh-bee, me, ice cream.
I like strawberry the best.
But Deh-bee doesn't.

After three days, I still hadn't heard from Chip. Obviously, his mother never told him about my visit. With everything unpacked and my room organized, I had time to ride my bike to town in search of friends. As soon as I reached Main Street, I spied Becky with her frizzy blond ringlets standing in front of the stationery store.

"Hey, Becky. I got back from California last week. You're the first person I've seen."

"Oh?" She looked at me kind of funny. Was there a bug in my hair or something?

I patted my head like I was smoothing it down from the breeze, just to make sure nothing gross lurked in there. "Yeah… I've been at the beach almost every day, but nobody's there."

"Which beach?"

"The Air Force beach. I—"

"Everybody's at the village beach. We don't walk all that way anymore." Her bangs covered one eye, and she brushed them away from her face. "Besides, *you're* the only one who came back."

She made it sound like I committed a crime by leaving in the middle of the school year. And worse, I returned.

"We came back because we like it here. Because… my friends are here."

Becky hadn't been a *close* friend a few months ago, but we hung out with all the same people. "You want to come over to my house? It's brand new. We built it so we'd have a place while my dad's gone."

I was begging her for a life preserver, s*omethin*g to let me know I wouldn't sink into a sea of oblivion like I did in Masterville.

Becky wrinkled her nose. "I don't think so. I'm supposed to meet Leigh and Melissa in front of the post office." She offered a smile tinged with pity. "Leigh is going with Chip now."

The last of my illusions flopped around gasping for oxygen like fish in a bucket. No wonder Chip's letters stopped. No wonder Leigh never wrote to me. All those tears when she said goodbye last March? They belonged to a crocodile.

The message was clear. No reason to further humiliate myself by begging to join them. But I wouldn't give Becky the satisfaction of seeing me cry *real* tears. "Guess I'll see you around."

"Yeah, see you when school starts." She pointed her bike toward the post office.

I glued a stiff smile on my face until Becky turned the corner. This was worse than California. My own friends acting like I was the "new person," except they already knew me. Even if they'd had my phone number, nobody would've called. What a fool I'd been.

Pedaling as fast as I could through the blur of tears, I made a beeline for home. A year ago, I would've run for comfort to my parents. Not anymore. For one thing, I only had one parent to run to. And Mom didn't need a blubbering almost-fourteen-year-old on her hands. If I ran to Grandma, she'd really make me feel like a baby. And that was the thing. I wasn't a baby. I was a teenager. Teenagers don't run crying to their mommies. Maybe to a best friend. But that was the problem. I didn't have one.

I dropped my bike on our front lawn and walked toward the duck pond. I didn't want to be with people. Let me die somewhere quiet. Alone.

It's tough to find an "alone" place in a beach town in the summer, but I stumbled onto one. Just before reaching the pond, land sloped upward from the bay. It had too many trees to be called a meadow, but the spaces were too open to be called woods. Clumps of bushes dotted the hill. No one seemed to be there. It was probably private property. Add trespassing to my list of idiocies.

Once out of sight from the road, I sat with my back against a small tree trunk, still too exposed to anyone who might walk by. An opening underneath the clump of bushes opposite me attracted my attention, beckoning. The natural arch was just high enough and wide enough to allow me to slide in. Maybe I could hide from the world in there. I belly-crawled down the passage. Sunlight filtered through the leaves to create a green glow.

In the center of the clump, the path ended in an open space. Apparently, the bushes grew in a circle, and the branches met to make a dome high enough for me to sit. A miniature cathedral. No one could see me. I lay on the ground, curled up like a baby, and sobbed without sound.

Chip, the smart, good-looking, star football player. As his girl, everybody had accepted me. No wonder I'd been the only Air Force kid in the group last year. Mom had been right. Civilians didn't want to waste their time with Air Force brats who moved away. So, while I was gone, Chip replaced me. Not only had I lost a boyfriend, I'd lost a whole bunch of friends. Except they had never really been my friends, and I'd been too dumb to understand that. *Stupid, stupid, stupid Debbie.* Too stupid to listen to Mom. Too stupid to figure out people didn't want me.

Francie had moved to Idaho last month. She hated the place, and she missed Ernie, but at least he had stuck with her all the way to the day the family rolled out of the driveway. It turned out Chip was the wienie, not Ernie.

It was bad enough that my father was in danger every day. If he didn't come home, I would never smile the rest of my life. I shoved the awful thought away. It hadn't happened. But Chip's betrayal, and the double-cross from Leigh and Melissa? That *had* happened. How could I not think about it? Yeah, losing a boyfriend doesn't come anywhere close to losing a father, but once classes started, I'd see them all the time, a constant slap in the face. I'd feel the sting over and over. One hundred eighty-three days of school. Seven classes a day. Over a thousand slaps for the year.

I spent the rest of the summer babysitting Krista. Mom gushed about how I was such a wonderful, devoted big sister. She was half right. I loved Krista's company. But then again, what else did I have to do?

On a Friday afternoon, Krista and I stopped at the Sweetness Emporium. The sidewalk billboard advertised a special on my favorite ice cream flavor, butter brickle. For once, I had enough money.

To get to the counter, I needed to go up three steps to a deck, then walk between tables to a wall with an open window cut into it. Several girls from the high school worked on the other side of the window and took orders.

On this sunny afternoon, people occupied every seat. There was no way for me to get Krista's stroller up the steps and roll it between the tables all crammed together. I parked it next to the side railing, then led Krista up the steps with her clunky leg braces. As I tried to find a pathway to the counter, we step-slide-stepped our way on the outside rim of the deck. Eventually, we came to a dead end with tables placed against the railing. I'd have to forge a path.

Towing Krista behind me, I made my way between chairs until I reached one lady whose chair and backside were quite a distance from the table. She leaned forward talking to the friend facing her. A dozen blond braids intertwined all around her head, and long, dangly earrings flashed in the sunlight. Everything about her screamed "Hamptons Chic."

"Excuse me, may we get through?"

She didn't look up. Maybe she didn't hear me.

I repeated the question a little louder. "Excuse me, may we get through?"

She turned to regard the interruption. If anyone could look *down* her nose while looking *up* at the object of her disgust, this lady possessed the ability. "What is the problem?"

"My sister and I are trying to reach the counter." I spread one arm to indicate the crowd and nearly smacked a man in the back of the head at the next table. "Would you please let me by?"

One regal eyebrow rose. "Let you by?"

"Yes, ma'am. Could you…scoot in your chair…please?"

Her lips tightened, and she turned back to her friend. Was that a *no*? I waited. One more table, and we would be close to the order window. It would be hard to turn around, push Krista back through the crowd, and search for another path. We remained, inches from the woman, our presence like two skunks under someone's front porch.

Finally, she scraped the chair toward the table leaving us a three-inch space. My legs could just get by, and Krista was so skinny, I could easily drag her through. But I hadn't accounted for my own ample behind. It brushed against the back of the woman's head, and I messed up a couple of her braids in the process. *Oh, too bad.*

She scooted in another six inches in a hurry. "Sorry," I said. But I couldn't wipe the grin off my face until I heard her next comment.

"What was their mother thinking? That little girl should be in an institution, not in public." She crinkled her nose as if a child in braces should be avoided like dog doo on the lawn.

I didn't dare look anyone in the eye. Whenever I get this angry, Mom calls my expression the "Wicked Witch of the West." There's no hiding it. Daddy used to claim I could laser-blast people off the face of the earth. For the moment, I wished I could make Ms. Braids and Bangles disappear in a wisp of smoke. Instead, I stared at the counter and placed my order.

With ice cream cone in hand, I climbed over the deck railing. We weren't going back the way we came. Bracing myself against the rail, I hauled Krista over it, using one arm. It wasn't pretty, but I didn't drop her. Or the ice cream. Some of the customers smirked in amusement. Others pretended to ignore the awkward girl with her crippled sister.

When we reached the stroller, Krista clambered in on her own, oblivious to people's stares. As stone-faced as I could manage, I pushed her to the first corner, turned right, and stopped several yards down a quiet side street. Sitting on the curb, I shared my treat with Krista. The sour taste in my mouth ruined the sweet butter brickle. I pictured the cone mashed down on golden braids with melted ice cream dripping over dangly earrings and fake eyelashes.

If I had done that, maybe I would've felt better. At least until I got arrested. Or Mom found out.

Chapter 21:
Beaches

Big pool, big step. Oops!
Deh-bee grabs me, and I blink
Water from my eyes.

Melissa's mother invited us to the Marlin Club. Any other summer it would've been cool to have our choice of ocean or pool, plus lunch at a snack bar. Putting up with Melissa and Leigh for an entire afternoon took the fun out of it.

"Things have changed," I explained to Mom. "Chip is going with Leigh, and Leigh will probably be there with Melissa. They don't want me around. I don't want to go."

"I'm sure it's not that bad." She gathered our bathing suits and towels off the deck. "Just be friendly, and things will get better."

Mom was the one who had warned me this could happen, so why was she acting like it was no big deal? I tried another angle. "Remember our first few days in Masterville, and I said people in Hampton Shores were a lot friendlier than the people in California?"

"Mm-hm."

"And you said civilians don't like change, so they don't accept military people. They don't want to make friends with someone who is only going to move away. You said New York was no different from Masterville."

"Mm-hm." She looked around as if she'd lost something. "Would you pick up Wade's trunks on the ground? They fell off the railing."

I didn't move. "You're not listening! I'm trying to say you were right. Kids in Masterville knew we would move so they didn't get close. And now kids in town know I already moved once, and they don't want me either."

Mom folded a towel. "I'm listening, and I remember what I said. But I didn't mean that people will reject you. They just won't go out of their way to meet you." She pointed past the railing. "Please get Wade's suit."

I trudged down the three steps to the back yard. "I think you're wrong, at least about Melissa."

"Since you're back to stay, I think *you're* the one being too sensitive. If your friends liked you before you left, they'll like you now."

"Maybe they didn't really like me." I handed the bathing suit over the railing.

Her eyebrows rose in surprise, and then she offered that special "mom" smile. "Of course, they liked you. You're a sweet, kind, beautiful girl."

Every mother says things like that. I trudged back up the steps.

"Can we get a dog?"

Mom froze in the middle of stuffing a towel into the beach bag. "Where did that come from?"

"Dogs are good company. I'd never feel lonely."

She gave me that "you know better" look. "Grandma hates pets, and your sister is scared of dogs. Remember how she reacted at camp last summer?"

"How will Krista ever stop being afraid of dogs if she's never near one?"

"It's out of the question. Especially with your father gone. I can't add all the work of a dog."

She had a point. I sure didn't want to scoop poop every day. Once school started, I wouldn't have time to walk a dog. Would I have to shampoo him when he got stinky? Brush his teeth when he had doggy breath? And what if we ended up with a yapper? I hated little dogs that let rip a shrill bark at every enemy, real or imagined. I definitely wanted a *big* dog.

She tossed my bathing suit to me. "Get ready."

Oh, yeah. Our lovely beach club outing. Get ready for the next slap in the face, Debbie.

Mom tapped the back of my shoulder. "Go and join the group. You'll be fine." She pointed me toward Melissa, who stood in the middle of a cluster of girls from my class.

I shook my head. "I'll take Krista to the baby pool."

"I can take care of Krista. You've hardly taken time for yourself all summer. Go on."

She smiled, but her eyes commanded me not to embarrass her in front of Melissa's mom. Maybe Mrs. Martin was as clueless as my mother. Or was Mom having the same problem finding new friends and she wouldn't admit it?

With no more argument, I followed the group into the pool, a good little lemming. Everyone was *very nice*—while their mothers were in sight. When Melissa suggested we change into dry suits before heading out to the beach, it was a different story.

Our gaggle of sleek, towel-wrapped teens entered the locker room, beach bags dangling from wrists. Mine contained nothing but the clothes I needed for the drive home. It hadn't occurred to me to pack an extra suit. I didn't need two in one afternoon *last* summer.

Melissa barked orders like a sergeant during barracks inspection. "Becky and Liz, use dressing room three. Kelli and Joanne, use number four. Leigh and I will use number two. And Kelli, if you have that groovy psychedelic bikini, wear that one."

Kelli sparkled at the implied compliment. "It's my favorite, too."

"What about Debbie?" Joanne asked. "We can squeeze in three of us." She peeked behind the door of dressing room four. "I think."

Melissa grimaced in annoyance. When she made that kind of face, her smooth beauty fractured into little lines at the corners of her lips. Those would be a couple of deep, ugly wrinkles someday.

"It's okay," I said. "I didn't bring another suit anyway."

Melissa brightened. "Oh. Well. That solves that. We'll meet you out on the deck by the doors."

I took up my post where we had entered. After ten minutes, no one had come out. Were they putting on make-up or doing each other's hair? When I went back in to check, all three dressing rooms were empty, and the whole place was silent except for a cranky toddler being toweled down by his mom. Just to make sure, I explored all three aisles of the locker room and discovered—a second door.

Yup. It opened onto a different section of deck with the stairs up and over the dune just steps away. No one was waiting for me. No one had gone in search of me. One more slap in the face. Get used to it, Debbie.

I wandered back to the pool where Mom and several ladies relaxed in the sun, displaying various amounts of well-oiled skin in shades ranging from peach gold to glowing chocolate. Krista sat half-submerged on the steps of the pool with a variety of toys.

Mom peered at me over the top of her sunglasses. "Where are the others?"

I shrugged. "I don't know." I wasn't about to whine in front of the mothers.

Mom sighed.

"Can I take Krista on the beach?"

She frowned. "What time is it?"

I pointed to the clock mounted on a wall.

"Oh. I'd better get her dried off and dressed, and we'll get her home for a nap." She smiled at Mrs. Martin. "Melissa's mom has offered to let you and the boys stay, and she'll take you all home later."

Panic rose in me like a boa constrictor slithering up my body and squeezing… squeezing.

Krista chose that moment to slip on the step and slide into water over her head. Darting around Mom, I jumped in the pool and grabbed her, easily beating the lifeguard. With water streaming down her face into her eyes, Krista blinked at me. She didn't seem scared, only surprised.

Mom snatched her out of my grasp. "Are you okay, sweetie? Are you hurt?"

She grabbed a towel and roughly mopped the water from Krista's face. Maybe it was the shock of cold water followed by Mom's vigorous attention. Maybe her chin was still tender from when she split it open in the California pool. Or maybe it was an answer to my silent prayer for deliverance from an afternoon of torture, but Krista set up a wail. People could hear her past the deep end of the pool. No mother wanted to be the center of that kind of attention.

I held out my arms. "I'll get her into dry clothes. She'll calm down."

Mom didn't argue. She apologized to the ladies as I hustled Krista to Mrs. Martin's cabana. By the time Mom joined us, Krista was ready to go, and I had changed into shorts and a shirt. Mom didn't ask if I planned to stay.

Chapter 22:
Running Toward the Waves

Deh-bee's skin is red.
She almost drowned in the sea.
Is Deh-bee okay?

Although clouds threatened rain., Mom took all of us to the beach anyway. She liked the ocean even more than me, and with school starting soon, we wanted to spend every spare moment at the beach. The Air Force beach. When we arrived, no one but the lifeguard populated the shore.

The sea was rough. A red flag with a white circle whipped in the wind, a warning to weak swimmers. The hurricane hitting North Carolina was having its effects up here. Time after time, two waves, then three, rolled themselves into one as they crashed onto shore. The boys took one look, and with a whoop, ran for the water. The battle was on.

"Be careful," Mom called after them.

Rip currents wouldn't slow those two down. They knew how to escape by swimming sideways out of the current instead of fighting against it.

I stood at the water's edge. Sand from the ocean floor churned in the water, and yellow-brown foam rushed over my toes.

I was a good swimmer—in a pool. I could swim laps and tread water for hours. But ocean waves? While I nearly worshipped them, their magnificent power terrified me. I only went past breaking waves when the ocean was as calm as the bay. No amount of teasing from my brothers, no amount of shaming from Mom, not even Daddy's joking persuasion had ever gotten me to dive under a wave.

Paul tumbled in on a triple roller. Wade stood up from the same wild ride and shook seashell fragments out of his trunks.

"How bad is the undertow?" I asked. That was my other fear, getting dragged farther into the ocean than I wanted to go.

"Not bad," Paul said.

"Yeah, not bad," Wade echoed. "Even if you have trouble, the next wave will throw you right back to shore." He followed Paul into the roiling sea.

And I was left alone, abandoned to a solitary existence on the shore. Mom read a book in her beach chair. Krista filled a red bucket with sand, and the lifeguard had his eyes on my brothers.

A blue bucket lay on its side next to Krista. I tapped her shoulder, then pointed to the blue bucket. "Do you want me to fill it with water?" I signed "water" and pointed to the bucket.

Krista turned her attention back to the red one, shaking her head, and at the same time signing "no."

"Debbie," Mom's voice of warning.

Right. We weren't supposed to use signs. But

Krista was a lot happier when I did. Stupid doctor rules.

I stared at the waves, the mean, crushing waves. I watched my brothers who never questioned their ability to survive those vicious breakers.

The voice in my head taunted me. *How long are you going to be a wimp?*

I took a step forward.

"You're a strong swimmer." I spoke out loud, trying to gather courage.

Another step. Water swirled above my knees.

"If others can swim in this, so can you."

Third step. I staggered as the ocean surged to my waist.

"Time the waves." I remembered how I used to feel the rhythm of the jump rope before making my move to join the slap-slap of rope against concrete.

Three waves curled a few yards ahead. They'd knock me down once their combined force rushed me. I braced for it.

The water slammed me off my feet, and I allowed it to carry me to the ankle-deep wash. Scrambling up, I forged my way toward the waves until the sea convulsed in fury around my hips. *Do not give in to fear.* A double-roller headed my way. It broke, and in the second before it hit, I jumped, allowing my body to float on the rush of water instead of getting knocked off balance.

Almost to shore, I stood and faced the monster that stretched all the way to Africa. This was it. I was going to run toward the waves, time them, and *dive* just as they were ready to pulverize me.

But you hate going into water headfirst.

"Shut up!" I yelled at the stupid voice, and I yelled

at the breaking waves. "I either dive in, or I wipe out."

Without waiting for a cackling reply, I ran full-tilt into the whirling, swirling water. Its force slowed me to a determined slog toward the breakers. Three more waves piled onto each other.

Wait…

Wait…

Dive!

The surge passed above my body, then I aimed for the surface and popped into a world with a gray sky overhead and the next double roller beginning to curl. No time to think. Dive! Surface. Stroke toward the deep water, beyond the breakers—if such a place existed today.

Another triple formed. With strength I didn't know I had, I swam toward it and climbed the three ridges before they finished a curl. Was I almost to the calm? No. A huge wave crested in front of me. The water, now deeper than I was tall, didn't allow me to use my feet to push off for a dive. I kicked to a horizontal position and waited, then surface-dived before the wave hit. It caught my feet and dragged me back toward the shallows. I struggled to reach the surface. When I succeeded, I had just enough time to take a breath before getting slammed by the next roller. It smashed me to the bottom. Every inch of my exposed skin scraped against sand and shells as the tide shoved me to the beach. It stung, but it didn't kill me.

I stood once more, glanced at my chafed legs and belly, then turned toward the sea.

I shouted in competition with the roar of the waves. "You will never stop me. Never again!"

Splashing through the angry waters, I dove under

the next gigantic wave.

I. Was. Free.

I wrote a letter to Daddy telling him all about it. How I swam in a red-and-white-flag ocean and *survived*. How the boys asked me who I kept yelling at. How Krista pointed to my scraped legs, her eyes filled with worry that I was hurt. How Mom said I chose one of the worst days to learn how to swim in the ocean, and I told her it was the best day—if I could swim in that, I could swim in anything.

At sunset, I gazed out my bedroom window toward Vietnam, almost nine thousand miles to the southwest. The whole afternoon's battle with the sea had set me to thinking. Did Daddy have to overcome that kind of fear every day? He flew missions over enemy territory. Sometimes, he battled Soviet fighter jets. Pilots shot at each other with real bullets, not like when he practiced for war on American bases.

If I had gotten in trouble with the rough water today, the lifeguard would have saved me, but no lifeguard would pluck Daddy out of a burning plane. No one would throw him a life preserver and pull him to safety. But he was no wimp. He would meet danger head-on.

I slipped between cool sheets as night settled over Long Island. When it came to the ocean, I was no longer a wimp either. I'd silenced that nasty voice in my head.

If only facing old classmates could be as simple as facing the waves.

Chapter 23:
The Outcast Returns

I am not happy.
Deh-bee, Paw, and Way are gone
Again. I hate 'ool.

Last year, on the Tuesday after Labor Day, I started seventh grade. I entered a brand-new junior-senior high building and experienced changing classes and following a schedule for the very first time. I wore a red paisley dress, my first outfit in junior sizes. I was thrilled, terrified, and—I fell in love with Chip when we bumped heads reaching for things we had dropped under his desk.

Now, on the first day of school in *eighth* grade, I wasn't in love, I wasn't thrilled, and I was still terrified. But I'd been coaching myself for the last two weeks. I would start up a conversation with someone who wasn't part of the crowd I had run around with last year. Try to get to know them. Or talk to a new student. If there *were* any.

I dabbed "Pearly Pink" gloss on my lips and "Desert Rose" blush on my cheeks. How ironic. After four months in California wishing I were in Hampton Shores, now I longed to be back in the desert with Nora Jean. If it weren't for the ocean, the Mojave would be looking real good.

I examined my dress of gray and aqua swirls, two sizes larger than last year's, the result of growing five inches in twelve months. The last of my baby fat had traveled to other locations and created embarrassing curves. The dropped-shift dress did a reasonable job of hiding them. On impulse, I slung Nora Jean's beads around my neck. Maybe they'd give me courage.

Mom stood at the front door ready to see me off when I dragged myself downstairs. I heaved the large binder off the dining room table and into my arms, then struggled with my purse to make sure I hadn't forgotten lunch money, lipstick, and an extra pen.

Mom gave me a squeeze and a kiss on the cheek. "You look beautiful."

"I look like a cow next to Melissa and Leigh."

Mom snorted. "Those girls look like sticks with legs. You want to look like Twiggy? Be thankful for that adorable figure you're growing into."

"I think I've grown past adorable, and I'm moving on to *not*-so-pleasingly plump."

She stepped back and squinted. "You look perfect to me, and the blue and green necklace really makes the outfit. But if you're worried about getting fat, stop eating candy and potato chips."

Right. Nobody was going to feel sorry for me, except me.

I walked into the familiar building, my heart thudding so loud it competed with the hubbub of six hundred kids cramming themselves through the array of doors. With no Chip at my side, no one in the sea of faces came up to say "hi" to the new-old nobody.

My homeroom, last names F through H, was three doors down from the one I had in seventh grade. The nameplate on the door read, "Mrs. Kandiss. English Department." She wasn't here last year. I hesitated and peeked in before walking through the door. A young woman stood behind the teacher's desk--a Barbie doll in a librarian's outfit. She wore a prim skirt and blouse, sensible pumps, and black-framed glasses that came to a point like Cat Woman's mask. Her platinum blond hair was swept up in an old-fashioned French twist, which was the only reason I didn't mistake her for an over-dressed high school student. She had to be *very* new. I returned her quiet smile with one of my own.

Assigned seats had been placed in alphabetical order, as usual. The front corner desk nearest the door contained Sam Farmer's name, and I bet if I went to the far back corner desk, I'd find Liz Hull's schedule. Hansen was probably close to where it was last year, and I'd be sitting behind Chip again. Awkward. At least Leigh's last name ended with M.

Moving to the fourth row from the door, I read the name on the front desk. Maureen Godby. I followed the desks toward the back wall. Amy Guthrie, Charles Winthrop Handlon (Chip), Veronica Hanks, Deborah Hansen. *Veronica Hanks?* Somebody new would be a buffer. *Thank you, God.* I perched on the edge of my seat and slid Nora Jean's beads around my fingers. I could do this.

Even though I knew almost all of the kids as they entered, nobody said a word to me. Girls chattered at each other. A couple of guys nodded their recognition. Sally Hendricks, who never said anything in class, looked at me like a mouse who'd discovered a cat within pouncing distance. What did I ever do to *her?* Even Marty, who used to tease me all the time, just gave me a wink but no sass.

Was this going to be my life for the next five years? Go to class, sing in choir, eat lunch, go home. All in a silent bubble?

Chip entered. He was over six feet tall now, all arms and legs. His large head seemed ready to bobble off his skinny neck. He reached his seat and didn't look my way.

Come on, Debbie. Talk to somebody.

A skinny little girl who really did look like Twiggy passed the first desk in my row and said, "Hi, Maureen." She slipped into the seat in front of me. The new girl. Veronica. How come she already knew Maureen? Were they neighbors?

Veronica turned to me and smiled. Her long brown bangs pretty much covered her eyes *and* her cheeks. I was looking at a button nose poking out from a curtain of hair with teeth forming a wide smile. A real-life Cousin It from The Addams Family.

"Hi," the teeth said. "I'm Ronni."

A little of my nervousness drained away, and I managed a smile in return. "I'm Debbie."

"Are you new?" We both said it at the same time and laughed.

She answered first. "Not anymore. I moved here in April. My dad decided he wanted us to live way out of the City all year."

"City" as in New York City. Sometimes, the summer kids ended up living here year-round.

"I'm not exactly new either." I gazed around the classroom that was filling up with more noise by the minute. "We moved away in March and came back in July. My dad's Air Force."

Ronni nodded wisely, then leaned over my desk to look at my schedule. "Deborah…Hansen." She looked up at me with a different kind of interest in her eyes. "Oh."

My rising hope for a new friend sank. What did "oh" mean? I'd better get ready for a triple-decker breaker of disappointment. And for just a moment, we'd seemed to be on the same wavelength.

Mrs. Kandiss rang the bell on her desk. The boys quieted immediately. They'd taken notice of the Barbie doll-teacher and aimed to please. The girls' chatter subsided slowly. Before Ronni turned to face the teacher, she whispered, "We'll talk after homeroom."

Maybe all was not lost.

Chapter 24:
Ronni

*When will Deh-bee get
Home? Oh! She is in the park.
She has a new friend.*

As Ronni and I walked slowly down the hall toward first period history class, we compared schedules. We shared history, third period math, and sixth period English—with Mrs. Kandiss. But we didn't have the same lunch hour. Kids streamed by us. We ignored them. They ignored us.

"Maybe I should join the choir and forget my art class." Ronni studied her schedule once again. "Then we would have another class together *and* lunch."

"Will they let you do that?"

"Probably. There's just one problem." The broad smile returned, except this time she flipped the bangs off her face, and her eyes sparkled. "I can't sing."

"Lots of people say that, but they carry a tune just fine."

"Not me. I sound like a donkey." She started singing an old Beatles song. "She loves you, yeah,

yeah, yeah."

She truly was awful. All the words landed on the same note, sort of, and she ended with some kind of hoarse, barking sound.

I stopped in the middle of the hall, and others paused to stare.

Ronni bowed. "Have I made my point?"

I didn't know what to say and still be kind.

"It's okay. You're allowed to laugh." Then *she* laughed, probably at the stunned look that had to be on my face.

She grabbed my arm and pulled me toward our classroom. As we entered, I finally came up with a response to her performance. "Are you any good at art?"

"Better than singing." She dropped her books on the first open desk. Flipping open a notepad, she showed me some pencil sketches. She had the usual fashion models we all tried to draw, but further pages displayed an adorable puppy peeking out from behind a bush, a sailboat bobbing on a lake, and the New York skyline. She was good. More than good.

"Stick with your art class." I pointed to the puppy's eyes. "How do you give him such a playful expression?"

"I don't know. I just start drawing." She closed the sketch pad. "But I do know you won't drop choir."

I jerked my attention from Miss Selkirk's welcome note on the board. "How do you know that?"

She inclined her head toward Melissa, who had taken a seat on the opposite side of the room. "She had the lead in the musical last year. Other kids told me you would've done a much better job."

"Really? They said that?" I wished someone had told *me.*

Leigh passed behind Ronni on her way to Melissa. When our eyes met, she raised her eyebrows, a haughty Jezebel. Eavesdropping?

Ronni noticed my distraction and turned to check it out. Her gaze followed Leigh's progress. "Don't worry about them. It didn't take long for me to figure out they stab a *lot* of people in the back."

I didn't want to cry in the middle of a crowded classroom, but I got the feeling Ronni wouldn't look down on me if I did.

The rest of the day went okay. It felt good to be in choir again. Mr. Basso started out with his corny joke about how he sings tenor, not bass, and somehow, he got all of us to sound really good for a first rehearsal.

Lunch was the worst. I sat with some seventh-graders from the base, but all of the eighth-graders I knew had moved. Jimmy Pulizzi's dad should be finished with his tour of Vietnam around Halloween, which meant Jimmy would be able to move out of Queens to their next assignment before Christmas.

Sixth period English was the high point. Not only was Mrs. Kandiss as nice as she was gorgeous, but Ronni and I discovered we're both walkers, not bus-riders. We agreed to meet at our lockers right after school, which really gave me something to look forward to after a dismal gym class.

"Here." Ronni waved a piece of paper under my nose.

"What's this?"

Her Cousin It smile appeared again. "It's a portrait of Melissa and Leigh. I thought you'd like it."

I pinched one corner of the paper to take it from her, like it had germs on it or something. Titled, "The Best of the Back-biters," Ronni had drawn two sharks with flowing hair, eyes dolled up with thick lashes and green eye shadow, and full red lips above jagged teeth. With a few extra lines, she had managed to show Melissa's arrogant pout and Leigh's lapdog expression.

With snide satisfaction, I handed it back to her. "Brilliant."

"Keep it. I drew it for you." She held out the page.

"If anybody sees this in my possession..." Being ignored had to be better than turning myself into a prime target for revenge. "I think it's safer in your portfolio."

"Chicken." She winked at me.

"I'd rather be a live chicken than a dead duck."

She heaved a heavy, fake sigh. "Okay. I'll keep it." And she slid it into her sketchpad.

It turned out Ronni's place was on my way home. She only lived two blocks from me in a tiny cottage. Roses lined the front porch, and all kinds of flowers surrounded the back patio.

"My mom's favorite activity," Ronni said as we observed the clumps of color dotting the yard. "I think it's the real reason we moved here. If only she could cook this well."

"It's beautiful." I could pretend I was a princess hidden away in a magical forest glade. A kind, handsome prince would discover me, and we'd live happily ever—I cut off my imagination. I was almost fourteen, not six.

After I met Mrs. Hanks, a tiny lady—I could see who her daughter took after—Ronni showed me the room she shared with her younger sister, who was in seventh grade. "Sorry about the mess. Vicki is a slob."

The beds weren't made. Clothes lay crumpled all over the bed, dresser, and floor. Grandma would have a royal fit if my room looked that bad. She got upset if I didn't remove the scrap paper from my little trash can once it became half-full.

Ronni bounced onto her bed, at least I assumed it was her bed. I didn't know where to sit so I stood on a circle of unlittered floor. She bounced up again. "It's too stuffy in here. Let's go for a walk."

"I'll show you how to get to my house," I offered.

"Sounds good."

As we walked, her one-syllable comment from the morning still echoed in my mind. "What did you mean when you saw my name on the schedule this morning, and said 'Oh?'"

"Oh," she repeated. "I wasn't sure what to think yet. I should've known."

"Known what?"

"That Melissa lies all the time."

"She lied about me?" Was there more to everyone's *un*friendliness than my absence since March?

"I didn't know it was a lie when she told me. I'd never met you, so how would I know?"

"What did she tell you?"

"Well, she told everybody. I just happened to be there."

With each sentence Ronni had spoken, I'd walked

faster until I'd picked up my pace to a New Yorker speed-walk.

"Hey, slow down. I'm short, you know."

"Sorry." We reached the park across the street from my house. No one played there at the moment. "Let's sit over here before we go to my place. You have to tell me this whole story."

I showed her a tree with the perfect branch that was only three feet off the ground. I couldn't climb a tree to save my life, but I could at least sit in this one. We made ourselves comfortable, me with my back against the trunk, Ronni leaning on the branch as it rose at an angle. Our legs dangled on either side, like we were riding a horse.

"So, what did Melissa say about me?"

Ronni stretched and plucked a leaf from a twig above her head. "I guess when everyone said you would have been great in the starring role of the musical, it hurt Melissa's feelings since *she* was the star. She said you were so stuck-up and never talked to anybody, and that the rest of them weren't worth your time. Would they rather have *her* in the lead role, who at least talked to people, or a snob like you? Obviously, I didn't know anything about the show. You know, me and singing?" She gave me her Cousin It grin again.

I offered a smirk in return, but how could I defend myself? I didn't talk to people because I never knew what to say. Most of the girls liked to talk about the latest fashions, but I didn't know much about that stuff, especially since my figure was obviously gearing toward Jane Russell of the 1940s than today's Goldie Hawn. Did that make me stuck-up?

Ronni filled in my silence with the rest of the

story. "Then Leigh added her two cents and said you'd promised to write, but no one had heard a word from you, so you were probably off gallivanting with movie stars in Hollywood." She flipped her bangs out of her eyes. "*Gallivanting*. She actually used that word. Which is when I stopped listening. Who'd believe that an Air Force kid would be accepted into any kind of Hollywood crowd?"

"Yeah, if I can't get into the Hamptons crowd, what are my chances with Hollywood?"

She laughed. "Anyway, once I saw you were the *infamous* Debbie Hansen, I said, 'Oh.' Just remember, I always thought Melissa and Leigh were lying."

"But you wanted to make sure for yourself."

"Well, yeah." She swung one leg over the branch and hopped off. "It didn't take long. You talked to me right away, didn't you?"

"So, I'm not a snob if I talk to you?"

"Didn't you see that no one from that group talked to me?"

"You said hi to Maureen."

"Did she say hi back?"

I tried to remember.

"Exactly." Ronni nodded as if she could read my mind. "But you immediately asked me if I was new."

"That's because I've been new so many times, I really want to be friendly to other new people. I know how it feels. But I'm shy. It's hard for me to do that."

"Yeah, I could tell. Can you tell that I'm *not* shy?"

I slid off the branch. "I think I've figured that out."

We strolled across the street, and I opened the front door. "Just so you know, by the time you got to Hampton Shores, I had written two letters to Chip, and one each to Leigh and Melissa."

"Not surprised," said my new best friend.

Chapter 25:
Man of the House

I get so angry.
Nobody understands me.
Then Paw got mad, too.

Paul was driving me crazy with his *Father Knows Best* routine. Last week, Roy, a guy in my class, came to the house to hang out with me. My first inkling of hope for a dating life. Paul followed us down the block when we left for a walk.

I spun to face him. "Will you leave us alone and go home?"

He didn't say a word, just watched us keep walking. When I looked back again, he was still behind us about a half a block back.

Mom said it was kind of cute. Right. Roy didn't call me again. Did Paul plan to run off every guy who showed interest? Next year, we'd be in the same school building. I'd never be rid of him.

Wade was mad at him, too. Instead of the normal big brother banter, Paul ordered him around like a general with the troops.

Then Paul tried out his parenting skills on Krista. As Grandma and I cleared plates from the table and Mom scooped ice cream at the kitchen counter, Krista jabbered at the boys, trying to tell them something. No one understood what she wanted. In frustration, she threw her hands into the air and clipped her plastic cup of milk on the upswing.

Paul slammed his fist on the table. "Krista!"

Like she could hear him.

She felt the vibration through the table, though, and she could see the ugly expression on his face. Her own face registered shock as she realized his anger was aimed at her.

"Bad girl. Look at this mess." Paul pointed to the puddle of milk threatening to become a waterfall off the edge of the table. "Go to your room."

He started to lift Krista from her chair when Mom intervened. "Paul Grant Hansen, what do you think you're doing?"

"She got mad, and she spilled her milk."

"Yes, she did. But I asked what *you* were doing."

"I'm—" He stopped and looked from Mom to Krista. His eyes questioned Mom as he settled Krista back in her chair and returned to his seat.

Mom's voice gentled. "You're trying to be the daddy, Paul. And you're not. And that's okay."

"But Dad's not here."

"No, he's not. But you don't have to do his job."

Paul frowned and opened his mouth to object.

Mom spoke first. "I appreciate all the man's work you do around here. You're only twelve years old, and you mow the lawn and help out whenever I ask. You and Wade both. I can't think what I'd do without all three of you helping around here.

"But only your dad can be Krista's daddy. Nobody else. And you're Wade's big brother, not his father. You're Debbie's *little* brother, not her appointed guardian." She walked around the table to where he sat. Placing a hand on Paul's head, she ruffled his hair. "I have no complaints on your brother skills. Keep being a good brother. You don't have to be a father."

Paul stared at his plate. His lip quivered. "May I be excused?"

"Certainly." She squeezed his shoulder, and he ran from the room.

Paul *never* cried. Now, I wished I'd been nicer when he tried to protect me.

Mom looked at me and Wade. "You're excused, too. We'll save the ice cream for later."

We pushed away from the table, not sure what to say or do. And what was Krista thinking? First, Paul was angry with her. Then Mom and Paul seemed angry with each other. Then they both looked sad until Paul ran away. And whatever Krista had wanted to tell us never got communicated. Did it matter to her?

Grandma left the dining room and returned with dish towels to mop up the rest of the milk. She hadn't said a word. As I shuffled out, Mom asked her, "Did I do the right thing?"

Grandma murmured a response that faded as I headed upstairs. "Little boys can't take on the burden…"

Saturday afternoons during football season were the best. I usually didn't have a ride to the away games, but if they were at home, Ronni, my brothers, and I walked to the school, stuffed ourselves with popcorn from the concession stand, and cheered on our lousy team. Wrestling was king at the high school. Football, not so much. So far, our record was one win and four losses.

I didn't care anything about football, but Bill Neagley was on the team. Auburn hair, dreamy brown eyes. He was the back-up fullback and only in ninth grade. He didn't know I existed, but I went to every home game in the hope that he'd get his big chance on the field.

Today's game was special. Homecoming. We always played Southampton on Homecoming Day, and we always lost. The old football players from years ago got honored, and we had a coronation ceremony for the Homecoming Court. The seniors, Cammie Tillman and Kenny Meyerholtz, were crowned king and queen. Bill was the freshman prince. There would be a big dance tonight. Junior high not allowed.

The final score was 51-10, but the crowd flowed onto the field anyway—parents, girlfriends, classmates, little kids. I glimpsed Bill, who put his arm around Susie Halsey, another freshman. Ronni, in love with Roger Bechelman, had grabbed his wrist and jabbered away at him. He nodded absentmindedly and stared at the crowd over her head. Literally. There was a huge span of twelve inches between his six-foot frame and her pint-sized five feet.

A group of muddle-heads stood to my left. "Muddle-heads" was my own word for them. They were always talking politics and making no sense to me. Why they came to the game was beyond me. They hated jocks. They mocked high school traditions like Homecoming and graduation. They didn't have a good word to say about anyone over the age of thirty.

Artie Williams was their leader. He was a junior, he was big, and he was scary. If he didn't hate sports so much, he would've made a great offensive lineman. Maybe we could've won a few games.

I'd never seen him smile. He ranted on and on about the Black Panthers, like they were going to save the world or something. And he wasn't even black. Last year, he tried to have a sit-in at school to protest the Vietnam War. Only three muddle-heads joined him, and they all got suspended for a week.

This afternoon, Artie was in the middle of his group, glaring at the crowd, arms folded across his chest. Was he going to stage another sit-in? Would the muddle-heads march across the field with their arms upraised in a Black Power salute? His eyes lit on me. And stayed there.

"You!"

Like Dorothy when the Wizard of Oz commanded her to bring him the witch's broomstick, I trembled where I stood. If only I could run off the field the same way the Cowardly Lion ran down the castle corridor at the wizard's roar. But I was stuck in a crowd of people, frozen in place.

"You!" He bellowed again.

Ronni turned at the voice. Other kids looked his way, but his eyes remained on me. Why would he notice *me*?

"Debbie Hansen, right?" Angry dark eyes bored

into me.

I was hypnotized. Mute. A sacrificial lamb awaiting her doom.

"Right?" He added even more volume to his voice.

I nodded. Stranded. Trapped.

"You got a daddy in the *Square* Force?"

Ronni stepped closer to me. Other kids stepped away, leaving six feet of open space between me and Artie.

"He's in 'Nam, right?" He chuckled. An evil chuckle. "Cat got your tongue, huh? Don't want to admit your daddy's a baby-killer, huh?"

He couldn't talk about my father like that. "No. He's not." My voice shook.

But Artie was on a roll. "Kills gooks, doesn't he? Those people are just gooks to him."

"He's not like that." My voice firmed up, my hands became fists, but what could I do against a guy three times my size?

"Farmers in their fields, mothers in their huts, children in the river. He kills them all."

My whole body quaked, but I'd have my say, even if I ended up a bloody pile of bones in the next five minutes. *Use your diaphragm, Debbie. Project that voice.* "He's a pilot. He bombs railroads to cut off weapons from the enemy."

"There's people on those trains. Innocent people. But to him they're just gooks."

"Artie…leave the kid alone." Someone in the crowd offered a feeble protest.

Artie ignored my timid defender. "Her daddy's a baby killer. Hear that, y'all?"

Where were the teachers? The principal? The

parents who came to the game? On the far side of the field. Adults always drifted toward one goal post while kids congregated around the other.

Someone shoved me aside from behind, then stood directly in front of me like a shield. The back of his head looked familiar.

"You can't say that about my dad. Take it back."

Paul!

Another rustle from behind. "Yeah, take it back." Wade appeared beside his brother.

Artie laughed. "Look at these little guys. Whatcha gonna do, beat me up?"

Paul held up his fists in a boxer's stance. "Leave my sister alone. And shut up about my dad. You don't know anything about what he does."

Artie's eyes narrowed, and Wade raised his fists to join Paul's. All the kids near us had gone silent. Some of the guys shuffled closer to us. Maybe my brothers had shamed them into showing a little gumption.

Artie shifted his gaze to the solemn group. Five muddle-heads against fifty high school kids—which included the football team. If he thought about punching out two little boys, the silent, hostile students changed his mind. He shook his head and sneered. "Well, *I* ain't no baby-killer." And he turned and ambled away.

Ronni guided me to the chalked sideline where I sank onto the grass, unable to stop shaking. The other kids drifted away, a few of them mumbling apologies as if Artie's behavior was their fault.

Paul and Wade followed me, silent. I would never think of them as pests again.

"Thanks, guys."

Paul turned to face the nearly empty football field. "Let's go home."

Chapter 26:
Fatherless Christmas Eve

Fancy tree and gifts
For me. Lots of food and drinks.
Happy family.

Mom interrupted my Norwegian world of *Kristin Lavransdatter* by settling Krista on my lap. "We have too much to do before Aunt Viv and Uncle Hank get here this afternoon. Either clean all the bathrooms, help Grandma polish the silver, or watch Krista for me."

Easy choice, and Mom knew it. She kissed the top of Krista's head and left us in the den. The Christmas ham waited for her tender loving care.

I closed the book without complaining—peace on earth, goodwill toward men, and all that—and left my cozy spot on the sofa. I pulled out the Memory game from the cupboard next to the fireplace and motioned for Krista to sit on the floor. At two years old, she showed a talent for remembering pairs of cards. She could also sign numbers one through ten.

After three rounds, we took a walk to the duck

pond in the icy breeze. Over and over I signed, "How many?" We counted cars and ducks and houses. Frozen, we returned home. Time for her lunch and a nap.

Once Krista had been put to bed, Mom handed me a dust cloth. "Living room and dining room. Family room if you've got time. They should be here in an hour."

I translated her instructions to: "Dust the living room and dining room at your leisure. Aunt Viv never arrives on time for anything, so you have at least an hour to read. Then amble into the family room and see if you notice any dust on the mantle. No? Go back to your book. Read until Krista wakes up or the cousins arrive."

Three hours later, Mom was tying the bow on Krista's Christmas dress, and I'd done all my chores, dressed for a fancy dinner, and finished my book when the doorbell rang. Hugs all around as Grandma collected coats and Uncle Hank set a mound of packages in front of the tree. We'd broken with tradition. This year we had decorated the seven-foot spruce a day early.

"Oooooh! The house smells like Christmas!" Aunt Viv inhaled deeply and closed her eyes in a mock swoon. "Ham and clove and the scent of pine all mixed into one delectable aroma."

She swooped down on Krista and scooped her up in a smothering hug. "Look at you! What a big girl! What did you tell Santa you wanted for Christmas?" Relaxing her grip, she peered at Krista. My sister's eyes reflected a panicked "get me out of here" expression, but her mouth offered a be-nice-to-this-crazy-lady smile.

Timmy was my age and eagerly followed my little brothers to the den to watch football. Nadine was sixteen. For the last couple of years, she hadn't bothered to hang out with the *little* kids. She sat with the grown-ups during their cocktail hour and wrapped strands of her sleek, dark brown hair around her finger while she daydreamed about her latest boyfriend. At least that's what I assumed. Either that, or she was practicing her understudy hopes for Agent 99 from *Get Smart.*

I had a choice. Watch college football in the den with the boys, or stay with the adults and listen to church gossip, family gossip, and my aunt's business success—or flop—depending on her latest inspiration. Unlike high school games, football on TV was boring. I decided it might be worth listening to Grandma and Aunt Viv. Besides, bacon-wrapped water chestnuts lay within my reach if I stayed with the adults.

Poor Krista's choices were worse. She could watch a bunch of figures running around banging into each other on the television, or she could watch the people in the living room move their lips. If she tried to touch the pretty packages, some adult would remove her from the temptation. She opted to join the boys.

The subjects of Daddy and war seemed to be off limits, so I was treated to some fascinating information as I sipped ginger ale and sidled closer to the bacon wraps.

"How are you enjoying your new home, Judith?" Aunt Viv inquired of Grandma.

"The house is lovely, but the stairs are a bit of a concern." Grandma looked down at the high-heeled shoes she'd worn for holiday company. "Between my bunions and a touch of arthritis, I try to limit the up and down to once or twice a day."

Aunt Viv clucked her tongue in proper sympathy. "Not to mention the threat of slipping on those stairs. You could break a leg!"

"I'm very careful. Years ago, I broke my arm in just such an accident."

"A broken arm! Oh, how painful!" Aunt Viv was all exclamation points this evening. "I broke my arm last spring when I tripped coming off the subway. It's still sore." She rubbed her left forearm as if the gentle massage would soothe the months-old pain.

I turned my attention to Uncle Hank and Mom, but she was asking him about his job in finance, and I didn't understand his mumbled, one-word replies. Which left me with Nadine. I gave her a wide smile and nodded several times. A nervous bobble-head doll. Small talk made me nervous, I guess. "How's school going this year?"

Nadine was so pretty, she had to be one of the most popular kids in her class. She flicked her hand like school was no big deal. "Boring. One more year after this, and I'll be done."

"No college?"

She shrugged. "I'd rather get a job in the City. Gary will be playing basketball at NYU, so that will be cool to go to all the games."

I didn't want to be rude and tell her "Fat chance" of having the same boyfriend in two years, so I remained silent. And I couldn't think of anything else to say. She droned on about Gary's fantastic stats, number of baskets, number of assists... Krista had made the better choice.

Finally, it was time to eat. The sun of a pineapple-glazed ham dominated the solar system of lesser dishes. Almost a dozen platters overloaded our expanded dining room table. But who would pray the blessing? Daddy always did. We glanced at each other uneasily.

Mom smiled at Uncle Hank. "Would you do the honors?"

With much clearing of his throat, Uncle Hank bowed his head. The rest of us followed his example. "Lord, we thank You for this feast before us, for Your goodness in sending Your Son to save this world. We lift up my brother Grant to You and ask for Your protection upon him. Bring him home safely to his family. In the name of the Father, Son, and Holy Spirit. Amen."

For Uncle Hank, who rarely put five words together, it was a great prayer. And it seemed to break the ice on the forbidden subject of the person missing at this Christmas feast. As Uncle Hank sliced the ham and we passed Aunt Viv's sweet potato casserole along with all the other choices, the "remember when" conversations flew across the table like sparrows crisscrossing telephone wires. Daddy played the starring role in many of those stories. Howling at the moon on the beach. Sitting on the splintered sled. He turned red from laughing so hard every time he heard it. The terrifying hayride. Timmy didn't appreciate the humor at his expense.

Krista sat in her highchair in the corner closest to Mom to save space for the extras at the table. Mom kept refilling Krista's plate with ham and potatoes and green beans, but nobody talked to her. She sat there, behind the rest of us, watching ten other people move their lips in dozens of conversations. I leaned back to catch her attention. She grinned at me, mouth filled with mashed potatoes. What a little sweetheart.

I smiled back and signed, "Good food?"

She wiggled her fist up and down for "yes" and stuffed another full spoon of potatoes into her mouth.

Had Mom noticed our sign language? No. She was handing the ham platter to Paul.

I returned to school-talk with Tim. Then *I* forgot about Krista, too.

By ten o'clock, we'd all opened our gifts from Uncle Hank and Aunt Viv, the kitchen had been cleaned, thanks to Nadine and me, and my cousins were on their way to the Christmas Eve service in Garden City.

Mom collapsed on the living room sofa. "Give me a minute, and I'll get Krista to bed before we haul out the rest of the presents."

"Can we get everything under the tree and the stockings filled before it's time for church?" I asked.

Mom stared at me as if I'd lost my mind. "You want to go to church?"

"Yes! We always go to church. You and Daddy and Paul and me. And this is Wade's first chance to go to the midnight service."

In our home, ten years old was the magic age for attending the special, late-night service. I'd fallen in love with it.

After we sing Christmas hymns and participate in Communion, the lights go out. The pastor touches a flame to one candle. One little light in the entire church. Then he moves to a person in the front pew and lights the candle he or she holds. Two lights.

He moves across the aisle and lights the candle of the person on the end of that row. Three lights. Then each person shares their candle with the person next to them, the last one passing light to the row behind, until the entire church glows.

Silent night, Holy night, Son of God, Love's pure light.

Every year, I cry at the beauty of it. And for the meaning behind it. Share the Light of Christ to one person at a time until Jesus glows across the world.

And Mom didn't want to go? I'd waited all day for this!

"Debbie, I'm beat. It's been a long day. We're going to have to skip it this year."

"But I wanted to pray for Daddy there. Because he probably went to a church service too, and prayed for *us*. And it's a beautiful place to pray."

Mom hesitated. "By the time we get back, it will be after midnight. And I still haven't put presents under the tree or filled the stockings or put our special breakfast together."

Tears clogged my throat, and I appealed to my grandmother. "Grandma, would you take me?"

She moved to tuck me under her arm, but I'd grown too tall. "I really abhor going out in this weather, especially at night."

"I don't mind missing one year," Paul said. "I can do the presents."

"But I'll have to show you where they're all stashed," Mom said.

Paul grinned. "I know where they are."

Mom raised an eyebrow.

"Under your bed, in your closet, in a big box in the

corner of the basement, and I'm guessing Grandma has the rest."

"And I suppose you know what's in them, too."

Paul rounded his eyes in an attempt to look innocent. "I've guessed some of 'em."

I glanced at Wade who was contemplating the floor. If he said his heart was set on it, we could probably persuade Mom together, but if he chose to stay home, I'd be outvoted.

"I kind of wanted to see what it looked like in church with a bunch of candles…" He met my gaze. "But I guess I can wait one more year." He offered a shrug of apology, knowing he'd been my last line of defense. "They'll have a midnight service next year. Besides, this is my only chance to play Santa Claus."

Crying or sulking wouldn't help me now. I wouldn't get to bask in candlelight and think about the meaning of that Baby in the manger. It was just…sad.

Grandma patted my shoulder. "If your mom is willing to take you to church, I can get Krista to bed, and your brothers and I can deal with the presents." She gave Mom the classic mother-to-daughter look. "Breakfast can wait until morning."

Mom nodded. Krista was curled up on the sofa watching us with sleepy eyes. Mom knelt beside her. "Grandma will help you with pajamas. Debbie and I are going to church."

While she spoke, she used her hands—pointing to Grandma, pulling on Krista's clothes, and carefully mouthing "pajamas" so Krista could *see* the word. Mom pointed to me and herself, then made a driving-with-a-steering-wheel motion, then showed praying hands for church. It wasn't real sign language, but it got the job done. Even Mom knew that forcing Krista to do nothing but read lips was dumb.

Krista yawned and nodded. Before I put on my coat, I carried her upstairs, and Grandma followed.

Mom and I exited church into a gentle, snow-globe world. The chorus of whispered "Merry Christmases" followed us out the door. Our boots didn't even crunch in the fluffy white cover on the pavement as we made our way back to the car. Since we had parked in the last spot next to the church's expanse of lawn, I stepped onto it and twirled, face to the sky. Snowflakes kissed my eyes and cheeks and melted on my tongue.

I'd sung my praises. I'd knelt at the altar, eucharist wafer in my hand, dipped it in the wine, and felt clean and pure inside and out. Mom had lit my candle, and I passed the flame to a lady I didn't know. We'd smiled at one another. I'd prayed for Daddy and for Jimmy's dad. I'd even prayed for Melissa and Leigh. Did either of them ever feel this peaceful?

I stopped twirling and opened my eyes. And there was Mom. Twirling. Face to the sky. Drinking drops of melted snowflakes!

When she opened her eyes and saw me grinning, she reached for my hand. For this moment, she looked like the relaxed, joyful mom I had known before Krista was born. Before German measles. Before hospitals. Before Vietnam.

"I'm glad we came," she said.

Chapter 27:
Fatherless Christmas Day

Wheels with brown ribbons.
Wheels go round and round. All they
Do is stare at it.

Christmas morning was almost as good as our other Christmases. I pretended Daddy was somewhere else in the house whenever I noticed him missing from all the fun.

After all the presents were opened, we enjoyed the egg casserole and sweet rolls, then Paul brought out the tape player. We settled in chairs and on the floor in front of the tree. Daddy rarely sent letters, but he did send audiotapes. Mini reel-to-reels. I liked to watch the tape run from one spool to the other as I listened to Daddy's voice. Later, Paul would remove the reel and put on a new one so we could record one of our own to send to Dad.

Usually, the boys reported all the news about sports and adventures in the woods behind our house. I updated him on my latest accomplishments at school. Mom kept her messages private. We always tried to get

Krista to talk into the microphone. She'd make a noise, and we'd applaud, but she didn't get it.

"It's going to take a little time today," Mom said. "I want Krista to be part of this, so every sentence or two we're going to stop the tape and tell Krista what Daddy said, whether she understands us or not."

Wade whooshed a sigh. I didn't think he could sit still for that long.

Every ten-seconds of conversation took a good five minutes to explain to Krista. Lots of times, we got lazy and didn't try. We could act out words like "eat" and "sleep," but there were just too many words, and I hadn't learned enough sign language. Even if Mom would let me use it. Life with Krista was a constant game of charades.

Daddy's tapes lasted anywhere from ten minutes to half an hour. Mom was right. This would take a while.

Krista had wandered over to the tree and pulled out her new board book to show me. I settled her on my lap.

"Merry Christmas!" Even Krista looked up as Dad's voice boomed out of the speaker and into her hearing aids. Paul quickly turned down the dial. "Do you have snow yet? I woke up to seventy-five degrees and sunny, with storms expected later this afternoon."

That seemed to be the weather every day at his home base in Thailand.

Mom stopped the tape and mouthed "Merry Christmas" to Krista, then fanned her face with her hand like she was really hot. She made her fingers wiggle in a downward motion to show the rain. Krista frowned in puzzlement.

"Daddy," Mom said. "Father." Krista could see

Father better.

Krista nodded wisely.

Daddy's voice continued. "We had a really yummy Christmas dinner in the mess hall. Spam turkey loaf, fake mashed potatoes, and creamed spinach."

"Oh, yuck," Paul grimaced.

Wade made a gagging motion with his finger in his mouth. Watching him, Krista screwed up her face in disgust.

"And something they pass off as apple pie," Daddy continued. "The crust was kind of gloppy, but it did taste like apples and cinnamon."

Mom stopped the tape.

"How do you describe spam turkey loaf?" I asked.

"I have no idea," she said.

"I know." Wade ran out of the room and returned with Krista's picture dictionary.

He found the picture of a cooked turkey. There was no picture of spam, of course, but he chose a loaf of bread instead. Showing Krista both pictures, he pretended to hold the turkey in one hand and bread in the other. Then he smashed his hands together like he had smushed the turkey and bread into one blob. Krista laughed.

"Dad ate that," Wade made the smushing motion again and put the "blob" to his mouth. "Dad--Father ate that." Then he held his nose with two fingers and made a sour face.

Krista laughed again, and we joined her. I didn't know if she understood, but she was highly entertained.

"Wait a minute." With a frown, I pointed at the tape recorder. "He had to send us this reel ahead of time so we'd get it by Christmas. He's making it up."

"Maybe they have a menu like we do at school," Paul suggested. "So, he really did eat turkey spam today. He just knew ahead of time."

"You're probably right." Mom leaned over and kissed the top of his head. "My logical genius."

Whether it was the kiss or the compliment, Paul turned a little pink.

Daddy went on to thank us for our gifts. We reminded Krista of the picture she had drawn.

"Father loves it. He put it on the wall of his room." I hugged myself to show love, plus Krista could read the word "love" on my lips. I acted like I was tacking the drawing to the wall. She smiled and hugged herself, too.

Daddy described the Christmas tree in the officer's club. They made it out of paper, then glued on paper ornaments and a paper star. We took time out from the recording to make our own paper tree so Krista could understand what Daddy just said.

Laughter filled his voice as he talked about the crazy Christmas jokes he and his buddies played on each other, but the more he went on, the sadder I felt. At least the rest of us had each other. Daddy didn't have any family with him, only the men in his squadron, who must be lonely, too.

He finished with the usual "I love you all" and added, "Happy New Year. When Christmas rolls around again, I'll be with you."

Mom turned off the tape. We sat silently, each in our own thoughts. Grandma dabbed at her eyes with a tissue. The boys wandered out of the room. Krista still waited for the final translation. How could Mom explain "next Christmas" to a two-year-old?

She tried to smile through pressed lips. After a couple of blinks, she pointed to Krista and held up three fingers. "When you are three." She pointed to the floor. "Father home."

Krista knew what a number was. She knew she was two years old, but did she have any idea how long until September? Daddy would get home before then, probably late June or early July. Whenever he completed one hundred missions.

Six months to go. Six months. Or forever.

Chapter 28:
Scream Into the Sea

My brothers are mean.
My sister won't play with me.
Da-di, please come home.

Only six weeks into the new year, and 1968 couldn't end soon enough. I had *tried* to be kind to Melissa. On our first day back at school after Christmas, I was standing behind her in the lunch line, and she had forgotten to bring money. I held out two quarters. I wasn't even going to ask for it back. A gift. Not a loan. She ignored my hand and called down the line, "Leigh? Anybody? Can I borrow enough for lunch?"

Forget *her*.

Whenever Mom got a phone call from some news reporter asking about Major Hansen's latest dogfight, she yelled at the guy, hung up, and then yelled at anyone in the house.

What did *we* do?

Grandma fussed at the littlest things. Today it was the laundry. I hadn't folded my sweaters correctly.

They were *my* sweaters. Why should she care if I folded them in half instead of in thirds?

Paul continued to drive me crazy trying to be my father. Wade was a pest. Krista's third temper tantrum of the day sent me out of the house.

I wanted to scream. Loud. Let it all out. Which was why I found myself walking in a cold wind—in my coat, scarf, and *no* mittens. They weren't in the closet, so I left without them.

Hands jammed in my pockets, I made it to the bridge in record time. The parking lot on the other side held one old blue car, its back end full of dents. Probably broken down and abandoned. As soon as I crossed the dune onto Lambert Beach, the wind slammed me backwards. Good. I wanted a fight. I lowered my head and charged toward the waves. They crashed against the shore sending up sprays of dirty foam. Tangle seaweed lay at the high tide line, smelling slimy and salty even in their frozen state.

I stood just beyond the reach of the last ripple. This was my moment. I looked around to make sure the beach was empty.

*Un*believable. A lone figure was walking in my direction. I couldn't let loose and scream now. Even though the guy couldn't hear me above the roar of the waves, I'd look like a crazy person.

I trudged toward him, pulling my scarf tight over my ears and wrapping the ends over my bare hands. The sooner we passed each other, the sooner I could get all the frustration out of my system.

As I got closer, I realized the guy was pretty big. Like football lineman big. Long hair whipped around his face in the wind. Was he some pothead? In a biker gang? Had I been stupid to come here by myself? *Don't stare at him, Debbie.*

Just as I was ready to pass him, he stepped into my path, and I hopped backward.

"Well, if it isn't Debbie Hansen, daughter of Square Force One."

Only one other person in town walking on the beach in February, and it had to be Artie. Well, he was going to find out this was not a day to mess with Debbie Hansen, daughter of a top dog fighter pilot.

"I came here to get *away* from people, Artie. Just leave me alone."

He mimicked me in a high voice. "Just leave me alone." With a scowl, he took another step forward. "You're the one invading *my* space. Maybe I wanted to be alone, too. Didja ever think about that?" He jabbed a gloved finger at my chest.

We were almost nose to nose, his face bent toward me, my chin lifted so I could look him in the eye. One more step and he would knock me down. I didn't care. There would be no more retreat. "So, keep walking. I'm not stopping you."

Glum despair replaced the fire in his eyes. He was the one who took a step back. "Only one other person on the whole beach in the middle of winter, and it had to be you."

"What have I ever done to you?" The scarf unwound from my hands when they gestured with the typical "why" motion. "What has my *dad* ever done to you?"

He shook his head and gazed down at the sand. "Nothing." Then he pivoted and faced the sea. "But I've got plenty against some other guys like him."

"Air Force pilots? What did they do?"

"They killed my brother." He kept his face toward the ocean, not watching to see how I reacted.

What did his brother have to do with fighter pilots in Vietnam? Was he fighting alongside communists in North Vietnam? That didn't make sense. But his brother was *dead*. And with that realization, everything about Artie's raging attitude made perfect sense.

I turned toward the sea, also. Two enemies, side by side, staring across the huge expanse of the Atlantic. This was where I came to talk to God—or scream out all my problems to Him, the One who created this amazing power of tides and waves and motion.

Did Artie come here for the same reason? Both of us on the beach on this day was no accident. I shivered. Not from the cold. Something important was about to happen. So I stood there. And waited.

More shivers. This time from the cold. My teeth started to chatter.

Artie looked down at me. "You still here?"

"I'm sorry about your brother."

"Yeah. Right." He turned his head away.

I waited, but he didn't say anything more. "What happened?"

He sneered at me. "None of your business."

"You hate me. You hate my father. You've *made* it my business."

"Okay." The fire was back in his eyes. "Two words. Friendly. Fire."

"In Vietnam?"

"Yeah. Jay was infantry. They never knew what was going to hit them. The NVA. The Vietcong. Hidden land mines. I knew he might not get back. But I never thought our own guys would strafe the enemy *and* brothers-in-arms."

"So, it was a mistake. An accident."

His glare fired thunderbolts of rage. "It wasn't an accident. Jay's captain called in the coordinates. When Jay's buddy came to visit us, he told me that. Only he and two other guys survived." He grabbed my arm. "What do you think of your precious daddy now?"

"My father wouldn't bomb his own guys, I'm sure."

No, I wasn't. Jay's captain had called for it. My dad would have complied.

Why would the captain have done that?

Artie let go of my arm with a downward jerk. "You're so sure you can't even look me in the eye."

"I'm sorry. I'm sorry! What do you want me to do?"

"I want you to hate this war, too!" He shouted into my face.

"You think I *like* this war?" I whirled around, took a deep breath, and *screamed.* It no longer mattered that I had an audience.

If I had felt like cutting loose when I left home, Artie had made it ten times worse. I didn't know why the captain had told the jets to bomb him. I didn't know if the pilots understood what their compliance meant for those below. I didn't know where to find answers. And God wouldn't tell me. I kept screaming.

Artie grabbed my shoulders and shook me. "What are you doing? Stop it."

"No. It's the only thing that helps." I inhaled, ready to let loose with another scream.

He peered into my face. Maybe it was the first time

he had ever truly looked at me. What did he see? A girl whose scarf had fallen to her shoulders, hair flying straight back in the wind, red nose, chapped lips, and she probably looked ready for a mental hospital. I screamed again, right into his face, the wind carrying the sound all the way to Montauk Point and beyond.

"It helps?" He sounded like a lost little boy.

Another scream answered his question. If Paul or Wade ever died in a war, I would be lost, too. If my dad died…

Artie let go of me and faced the waves again. He squared his shoulders, stared intensely at the horizon, and bellowed. A bull roaring out his pain.

I joined him. Two desperate kids screaming at the ocean, at God, seeking relief from a horrible world.

We walked back over the dune together.

"You were right." Artie's voice came out in a croak. "That helped."

I shrugged. "The pressure will eventually build up again, but at least now I can go home and not be a jerk to everybody."

Who cared if Paul wanted to be man of the house? He did that because he loved Daddy and didn't want to let him down. And if Wade always teased me or Krista? Maybe it was the way he showed affection. A stupid way, but I didn't have to get so mad about it.

"You're not even hoarse," Artie said. "I can barely talk."

"Breath support. I'm a singer."

"I'll need to figure that out for next time."

"Join the choir. You'll learn." I grinned at him.

Who would've thought I'd ever feel this comfortable with Artie Williams? Barriers get kicked down when you've screamed at the ocean with someone.

I adjusted my scarf. At least the wind was behind me on the way back.

"I'll drive you home," he said.

I wasn't supposed to get in a guy's car. The rule had been drilled in my head since I could walk. "Thanks. I'll be fine."

He grasped my hand and lifted it. "You're asking for frostbite. Another half hour out here?"

His broken-down looking car in the parking lot sat in the shadow of the dune, out of the wind. Tempting.

"The heat works good, too." When he wasn't angry, he looked like a nice guy. Messy hair, though.

The heater was one temptation too many. Getting home in five minutes, *out* of the wind, and *in* warmth.

As he pulled into the driveway, his face looked grim again. "I haven't changed my mind about the war, you know. If they draft me, I'll head for Canada."

"And I'll understand why." I fumbled with the door handle, my fingers still a bit numb. "Do me a favor though?"

"Maybe." His lips tightened.

"When the pressure builds up again and you see me at school?"

"Yeah…"

"Don't scream at me. Hold it all in until you can drive to the beach. *Then* you can scream."

He almost smiled. "See you around."

Chapter 29:
Plane Crash

Mah-mi, Deh-bee, and
Wam-mah at the food table.
Something bad happened.

The lilacs had blossomed already, and I walked home from school in clouds of their sweet fragrance. I should've been on the beach all day, not in a classroom. But school wasn't out for another month.

I waltzed through the front door, dropped my books on the stairs, and went in search of a snack. After that, I'd take Krista for a spin in the stroller. We could go back to Ronni's house where she'd been roped into helping with the garden. Maybe Krista could poke her fingers in the dirt, then Ronni and I would drop flower seeds in the holes.

I passed Mom and Grandma sitting at the dining room table.

"Hi." I grabbed the handle to the refrigerator. "As soon as I get changed, I'm going to Ronni's. Can I take Krista?"

Mom didn't answer.

I peeked around the open refrigerator door. Neither Mom nor Grandma ever sat around the house in the middle of the afternoon. "Is something wrong?"

Mom's back was to me. Grandma's eyes met mine, a deep V of anguish between her brows.

Daddy?

"What happened?"

Mom shook her head like she was trying to shrug off a bad dream. She turned in her seat to face me. Her eyes didn't hold the same intense pain as Grandma's. She seemed to stare beyond me. "Daddy… had an accident."

An accident? Did he have a car accident on the base in Thailand? A plane accident? When we lived on base, the sirens would sometimes sound in the middle of the day. All the off-duty pilots and airmen would jump in their cars and head for their battle stations if it was practice for a red alert. But if men didn't immediately react to the siren, we knew something bad had happened. Then the wives would wait to hear. Whose husband had crashed? Did he parachute to safety, or did he go down with the jet? Was he alive…or dead?

But Daddy was at war. Pilots in a war might get shot out of the sky, but they didn't have *accidents*. Right? I didn't allow my mind to ask the obvious question out loud. I froze, commanding my racing heart to slow down. Think nothing. Say nothing. Do nothing.

I stared at my mother. And waited.

Grandma touched Mom's hand. "Dorothy, tell her the rest. The poor child thinks he's dead."

Mom gave a start and looked back at her own

mother with a puzzled frown. She blinked as Grandma's words sank in. "Oh. Oh…"

With another little head shake, she turned her gaze back to me. "Daddy crashed. In a bad storm. He broke his back."

Last winter, a high school kid slammed his car into a tree and broke his back. He can't walk. He never came back to school. A tutor comes to his house.

Mom stared at the floor and frowned in concentration like I do when I'm trying to memorize a Bible verse for Sunday school, and I can't get the words right. "Dad called. He's going to be okay. He's in the hospital in San Diego."

She looked up then and smiled. It reminded me of Libby Woczieski's smile. Libby was the shyest girl in my class. Her smile always appeared both wobbly and hopeful.

"He said he might be able to recuperate at home. After a few weeks."

Her words slowly melted the frozen wall between my brain and the world. *Daddy's okay. Hospital. Coming home.*

Now I knew what *my knees turned to jelly* meant. I barely made it the three steps to a dining room chair before I collapsed into it. "So, he'll be home for good." Daddy might never walk again, but he'd be home.

Mom frowned again. Like my legs, her brain wasn't working up to speed. Maybe the three of us were sitting down because we all had jelly knees.

Finally, she shook her head no. "I don't think he'll be home for good. He still has to complete one hundred missions."

With a broken back? "How can he fly more

missions? Isn't he paralyzed?" No one in a wheelchair could fly a jet. Daddy wouldn't even be able to drive a car. Where would he work? How would he get in and out of the house? And we thought life was going to be different after Krista was born. This was worse.

Grandma cleared her throat. "He can walk. They call it a compression fracture. The spinal cord isn't severed."

"You know, like when you fall and land on your tailbone?" A bit of life entered Mom's voice. "Only this is worse. I guess the jolt from a crash landing can do that."

I pictured what I'd learned in science class about the human backbone. All those little discs with cushions of fluid between them. Like plates stacked together, each one sitting on its own pillow. If you drop the whole stack and they land hard enough, some of the pillows might slide right out with so much pressure. Then crash! Two plates smash together.

I got it. "When will he come home?"

Mom offered another Libby Woczieski smile. "I don't know. Maybe in a month? Seems to me like he'd stay in the hospital for a long time with a back injury."

"Are you going to fly to San Diego?" A romantic picture entered my mind with Mom hovering over Daddy in his hospital room. She'd serve him orange juice and fluff his pillows, kissing him before she sat in a chair beside the bed and read a novel out loud to ease the boredom.

"I wanted to, but your father said no. We'd drive each other crazy with him stuck in bed and me with nothing to do but talk him to death. Besides, it would be too hard for Grandma to take care of four kids."

As if to prove her point, she stood with renewed energy and then strode to the kitchen. As she furiously scrubbed the potatoes for dinner, she flashed me a bright smile. A little too bright. "I'm sure he's right."

No, he wasn't. Paul and I could've kept everything going when Grandma wasn't sure about stuff.

So much for romance.

Chapter 30:
Surprise

Hurray! Daddy's home!
Everybody is happy.
I smile all the time.

Two weeks ago, summer seemed to be on the way. Today, the poor lilacs were freezing their little blossoms off, and I didn't wear a coat this morning, so stupidly sure the sun would be out by afternoon. The stiff breeze off the ocean chilled me as much at three o'clock as it did on my way to school.

When I arrived home, a strange car was parked in our driveway. I hurried inside, too cold to acknowledge the man sitting in the living room with Mom. After dropping my books on the bottom step, I ran upstairs to change into jeans and a sweatshirt. Something fresh out of the dryer if I was lucky.

As I pulled on fuzzy socks, a familiar voice called my name from the bottom of the stairs. "Hey, Deb, aren't you at least going to say hello?"

Daddy?

I flew down the stairs.

He and Mom stood in the front hall. Before I could hurl myself into his arms, Mom stepped between us. Her simple motion got the message across. *What was I doing? My father had a broken back.* I backpedaled like Wiley E. Coyote on his way over a cliff. Unlike the cartoon character, I succeeded and came to a halt before I caused any damage.

Daddy looked awful. No wonder I didn't recognize him, but I couldn't wipe the grin off my face. Who cared if he was way too skinny, and his face looked gray and his hair had turned totally white?

He wrapped his arms around me in a firm hug as if to prove he didn't need Mom's protection. He kissed my cheek, and his lips remained pressed against my face. "I've missed you. All of you. So much."

Krista entered the room with a grin as wide as mine. Lucky girl. She must have enjoyed Daddy's attention most of the afternoon.

My questions tumbled out. "When did you get back? We thought it would be weeks. How much does it hurt? Do you have to do special exercises like Krista? Do you have to--"

"Hold up." A laugh rumbled from Daddy's throat. "I've already forgotten your first question."

Mom clucked at him. "Grant, sit down. You're not supposed to stand for long periods of time."

That answered one question I hadn't remembered to ask. He'd only been standing for two minutes.

"Let's all sit down." Mom placed a pillow behind Daddy's back as he eased into one of the living room's comfortable chairs.

Unnoticed by me until now, Grandma sat in its twin. I bounced onto the couch, and Krista climbed into my lap. Before she settled against me, I made sure she could see my lips. "Father home." I beamed at her.

She snuggled into me.

"What happened?" I asked. "Mom didn't think you'd be here for at least a month."

Mom answered for him. "He told his doctors he couldn't lie in bed for a month, so they let him come home. He took the first flight he could find, rented a car, and showed up on the doorstep at lunch time." She couldn't stop smiling. "I almost fell over when I answered the doorbell."

"You rang the doorbell to your own house?"

"Well, I wanted to surprise your mother, but I didn't want to scare anybody and just stroll in." He winked at Mom, whose cheeks turned rosy in response.

"The gentlemanly thing to do," Grandma said. "I'm sure I would have screamed to see a strange man in the house."

I lifted my chin, indignant. "Daddy's not a strange man."

"He was certainly an *unexpected* man," she responded. "He would have scared me to death."

Everything scared Grandma to death. She kept the doors locked in the middle of the day. Very annoying if I forgot my key, but she was forever telling me horrible stories of what she'd read in the *Daily News*. Like that would happen in Hampton Shores, almost a hundred miles away.

Mom tapped Krista's arm, trying to include her in our conversation. "Mommy surprised. Grandmother surprised to see Father."

She opened her eyes and mouth wide, and threw her hands up to show "surprise," which only gave the impression that an evil thug had jumped out from the shadows and threatened her with a knife. I could've shown her the real sign for "surprise," but why ruin the moment?

Pointing at Krista, Mom repeated her (terrified) "surprise" motion. "Were *you* surprised to see Father?"

Krista shook her head no. Sliding off my lap, she lumbered to Daddy with her brace-weighted legs. Mom lifted her onto his lap, and Krista gave him lots of kisses. The expression on his face looked like he'd found heaven on earth.

Paul and Wade barreled into the house. Like me, they almost missed the fact that people were in the living room. A quick U-turn brought them back.

"Whose car is in the driveway?" Paul asked.

"Daddy!" Lucky for Dad, Krista's presence on his lap prevented Wade from landing on top of him.

"Careful, Wade." Mom and Grandma instructed him together.

My husky ten-year-old brother dropped to his knees in front of Daddy and hugged his legs. Mom transferred Krista to her own lap, and Daddy leaned forward to ruffle Wade's hair.

"You came home." There were tears in Wade's voice. "You really came home." He straightened up and leaned against Daddy's chest.

"Of course, I came home."

"I thought they'd make you go back."

Mom and Daddy glanced at each other over Wade's head.

"How's about I get a hug from your brother, too?"

"Oh. Yeah." Wade stood. Daddy held a hand out, indicating Wade should take it and help him up. Wade braced himself and pulled. Daddy made it to his feet with no sign of pain.

"Thanks."

Wade stood a little taller.

Paul had remained in the doorway, silent. Daddy walked toward him. "Mom tells me you've done an excellent job as the man of the family. I'm proud of you, son."

Paul stuck out his hand. Dad shook it, then pulled him close. Paul never said a word, just hugged his dad like he'd never let him go.

Chapter 31:
Return to War

Everyone is sad
Again. I know what that means.
Daddy will be gone.

Dinner was better than a Thanksgiving feast. No time to thaw a steak or roast a turkey, but the spaghetti and meatballs tasted even better than a perfect, medium rare steak. Mom even made butterscotch sundaes for dessert instead of plain scoops of ice cream.

We laughed and shouted across the table, each kid trying to impress Daddy with the latest stories. Somehow, Mom got on the subject of unpacking Dad's suitcase and how awful his underwear looked. Paul, Wade, and I sniggered while Daddy turned bright red.

"I can't help how the local women on the base launder our clothes," he said. "I think they wash everything in the river."

Mom didn't see the humor in gray underwear. "We are replacing every pair. I'll go shopping tomorrow."

Krista looked at me, a question in her eyes. What

was so funny?

"Father's underpants," I said.

She frowned, not understanding.

The rest of the family moved on to other conversations. I leaned over and pulled at the waistband of her training pants. "Underpants." Then I pointed to Daddy. "Father's underpants."

A hint of a grin appeared on her face.

"Father's underpants. Ugly. Yucky." I scrunched up my face in disgust.

Krista giggled.

"Mommy says: buy more underpants. Buy new underpants."

Krista's face took on the now-familiar grimace of disgust when she couldn't connect with people. My words were beyond her understanding. Before a full-on tantrum erupted, I held up my hand in a wait signal and left the table. Running into Mom's bedroom—oh yeah, it was *both* parents' bedroom again—I grabbed the wallet out of Mom's purse and returned to Krista.

First, I showed her the wallet. Then, I acted like I was driving a car, my hands on the steering wheel. As the charade continued, I opened the car door, slammed it shut, and walked to one end of the room.

"What are you doing with my wallet?" Mom asked.

"Showing Krista something." I picked an orange out of the fruit bowl on the hutch, then took a dollar out of the wallet and handed it to an invisible cashier. I looked back at Krista. "Buy," I said. "I buy an orange." I repeated handing the money over.

Krista's lips made the shape for "b" and her mouth opened to an "ah," but no sound came from her throat.

"Right!" I grinned. "I buy the orange. Mommy buys underpants for Father."

I'd lost her again. She couldn't follow the string of words. This would be so much easier if I could use sign language. Except I hadn't learned "underpants" yet. I slowed it down with more motions while the boys renewed their snickers over the topic.

"Mommy…" I pointed to Mom.

Krista nodded.

"Buy…" I "handed over" the dollar.

Krista's one good eye focused on my motions.

"Underpants. *New* underpants." I plucked at her waistband again. Wade cracked up.

I walked around the table and plucked at the waistband of *his* underpants and then jumped away from the expected fist rounding in my direction.

"Hey!" He scowled at me.

I raised my eyebrows and gave him a lopsided smirk. "But you thought it was so funny."

I started over with Krista, who was grinning now. Good. She was beginning to get it. "Mommy." Point to Mom. "Buy." Hand over the dollar. "New underpants." I pointed to my own waistband. "For Father." I pointed at Daddy's waistband and plucked at his pants for good measure.

Everybody laughed including Krista, but I wasn't quick enough this time. Daddy grabbed my shirt before I twisted out of reach. When he plucked at *my* waistband, he dropped his hand and stared at me, an alarmed look on his face.

"You aren't wearing underwear?"

It was my turn to blush. "Of course, I am! But they're bikini style."

The boys laughed so hard Paul blew milk out his nose and Wade wiped tears from his eyes. They both used the tablecloth as a handkerchief.

Grandma rose from the table and began to clear the dishes. Tsk-tsking, she shook her head and muttered, "This is what happens when we cannot maintain genteel dinner conversation. Barbarians. Every one of you."

I folded my hands in my lap and pressed my lips together trying to look prim and proper. Wade caught my eye. My unladylike snort matched his which got Paul going again. Mom and Daddy exchanged glances and smiled as they shook their heads. We were a bunch of happy barbarians.

Krista stared from one person to the other, once again mystified by events. I'd finally gotten her to understand buying underpants, and now she'd want to know what the latest laugh was about. She'd have to wait until I could demonstrate bikini underwear in private.

I was *trying* to do homework upstairs in my room, but Mom's shrill voice carried clear across the house. "It's too soon to send you back. Two weeks! What are they *thinking?*"

Dad's words were muffled by the distance. He said something about not being cleared to fly.

"It's too soon. It's too soon," she repeated. "I'm going to call somebody in charge. There has to be a general with some sense in the ADC."

Something crashed to the kitchen floor. The phone? Did Daddy force it out of her hand?

His next words were distinct enough. "Cut it out, Dorothy. You know that's not going to do anything." A moment of silence. "Look. The sooner I go back, the sooner I get home."

My thoughts exactly.

"*If* you get back home."

That was it for me. Down the stairs and out the door. Paul and Wade were a block ahead, and I ran to catch up. At least Mom and Dad couldn't wake Krista from her nap.

The boys and I wandered as far as Turkey Bridge, a little beyond Wade's boundaries, but I figured it was okay if he was with Paul and me. For a Saturday afternoon in late spring, the bay was surprisingly empty. Only three sails zigzagged in the distance.

Wade kicked at a pebble in the road. "I don't want him to go back to the war."

"Nobody wants him to." I picked up one of the pebbles and dropped it over the side of the bridge. The pebble plopped into the water, creating a perfect circle of ripples.

"We knew he'd have to go." Paul leaned against the railing and stared across the bay to the opposite shore. "Let's just get it over with now instead of waiting another two weeks." He let his pebble fly with a flick of the wrist as if it would skim across the surface of the bay, but we stood too far above. It just disappeared into the water.

"But if he dies over there, we will have gotten two more weeks with him." Wade examined another pebble marbled with green. He pocketed it. "Mike and Pete Herzog didn't get *any* extra time. And their dad's not coming back."

Captain Herzog and another pilot in Daddy's squadron were killed in action. Why had God said no to *their* families' prayers?

I scanned the road for another colorful pebble like Wade's. There were several. They looked as if sea glass had found its way into granite. I chose three and handed one to Paul.

"What's this for?"

"Let's each keep one until Dad comes home again."

"Why?"

"They're pretty. And green is the color of life."

He shrugged. "And once he gets back?"

What *could* we do with four pebbles once he got back? "We give them to him. Kind of like a souvenir. We tell him the green stripe is why we kept them. And now that he's home we don't need them anymore." I paused, my mind filled with more possibilities. "Let's call them 'Life Stones.'"

"And what do we do with '*Life* Stones' if he doesn't come home?" Wade asked.

I couldn't look him in the eye, so I gazed over the railing. "Then we drop them over this bridge."

We walked home in silence, and when we entered the house, all was quiet. I found Mom, tight-lipped and grim in the laundry room.

"Where is everybody?" I asked.

"Grandma took Krista for a walk. Dad's picking up some last-minute items." She frowned at me. "Where were you and your brothers?"

"Walking around."

Mom sighed. "I'm sorry. It's okay now."

She didn't look like it was okay. Her swift, sharp movements in folding the laundry told me she was upset. Still, it *would* be okay. Mom would kiss Daddy goodbye tomorrow, and she wouldn't cry in front of us, at least not much, and she'd go back to being the Big Boss again until Daddy came home for good.

On Sunday, we went to church. Daddy was included in the list of prayer petitions, like he had been all year. Grandma had lunch waiting for us when we got home, but nobody felt like eating. Even Krista knew Daddy was going away again. She watched our solemn faces and asked no questions.

Daddy didn't let us drive him to the airport. He'd kept the rental car, so he and Mom wouldn't have to share the station wagon these past two weeks, and after lunch he loaded his luggage into the trunk. We camped out in the driveway and watched him. Krista pulled on my pant leg. Her lips formed an "oo," and she pulled on her waistband.

"New underpants?" she was asking.

I smiled and nodded. Yes, Daddy was leaving with new underpants. Not so funny anymore.

He slammed the trunk lid, and as a group we moved toward the front steps.

Daddy kissed Mom and pressed her close for a moment. Her lips quivered as a single tear rolled down her face.

He gave Grandma a gentle hug and a peck on the cheek. She patted his face and bestowed a kiss of blessing on his forehead.

He grabbed both boys and kissed the tops of their

heads while their arms created a double belt around his waist.

Then he wrapped his arms around me. I squeezed my eyes shut trying to keep the tears from spilling out and concentrated on memorizing the scent of tobacco and aftershave that made him Daddy.

He picked up Krista and planted a big kiss on her wet cheek. She cried soundlessly.

Sorrow had made us all mute.

And then he was gone.

As soon as he turned the corner, Mom looked at Grandma. "I'm following him."

"Of course, you are, dear." Grandma held out the car keys.

Mom accepted them, hugged Grandma tightly for a moment, and after wiping her eyes, she strode to the car.

Grandma stepped back inside. The boys ambled into the woods behind the house. Krista and I sat on the step looking in the direction where our parents had disappeared. When I got married, would I follow my husband as far as I could? I hoped so.

I had wanted to ask Daddy about what Artie had told me. Ask him about bombing our own soldiers. But I just couldn't do it. I couldn't put it in a letter last winter. I couldn't let him go back to war now, thinking his own daughter was critical of him. If he knew my doubts, it might jinx him. War movies always showed that if a pilot hesitated, he was done for.

I looked down at Krista. Her face showed no expression. What was *she* thinking? As I motioned for her to come inside, I pulled one of the pebbles from my pocket and gave it to her.

"For Father," I said.

Without trying to explain more, I led her upstairs to our room. A tiny crystal dish sat on my dresser. I dumped the mood rings out of it and replaced them with my green-striped pebble.

"Put your pebble in there, too." I pointed to the dish.

She obeyed with a puzzled frown.

I pointed to her, then to myself. "You. Me. We wait for Father to come home." I made the signs for "wait" and "home" and "Father."

Krista nodded. So far, so good.

"When Father comes home, we give the pebbles to him. Hurray! We will be happy!" I signed, FATHER-HOME-ME-GIVE, (hold up the pebble), and HAPPY.

Krista picked up hers, examined it, looked at me, and smiled. She signed, HAPPY. She understood. The best thing that happened all day.

Chapter 32:
Search for a School

Big, bad, mean lady.
Mah-mi did not let me play.
Big, bad, mean Mah-mi

At almost three years old, Krista was still in her Terrible Twos, throwing a tantrum every day. Some days more than one. If I couldn't understand what people said most of the time, I would have tantrums, too.

At least Krista knew a few things I was trying to tell her when I used sign language, but I never knew enough words to make things clear unless it was something simple like, "YOU? COOKIE?"

She needed to go to school, to be with other little deaf kids, and learn how to communicate without hissy fits. She needed Daddy. He'd always been the best at getting her to behave.

Some families had sent their deaf children to boarding school. Some of those kids weren't even two years old! Mom and Daddy discussed that possibility before he left for Vietnam. I would have run away from home if they'd sent Krista away. Well, I would've wanted to. It turned out they agreed with me. No boarding school for a toddler.

Mom decided to check out the Methodist preschool in town. It was close and not too expensive. Maybe Krista could go there once school started up again. If the teacher would take extra time with Krista, Mom said it would be perfect.

A tall, slender, middle-aged lady with gray streaks through her dark hair greeted us at the old wooden doors to the cedar-shingled church where the preschool had classes. Her smile froze in place as she watched Krista clomp up the steps in her leg braces.

"Mrs. Hansen, I'm Paula Denahy." Her arm was as stiff as the Tin Man's as she shook Mom's hand. "A pleasure to meet you."

"Thank you." Mom motioned for Krista to shake hands, too, but Krista just picked up a pebble off the step.

"And this must be Krista." Mrs. Denahy bent down to be eye level with Krista. "Hello, Krista."

Krista dropped the pebble and stared back. Her blind right eye slid closer to her nose, and she popped a thumb in her mouth. I hated to admit it, but my sister looked pretty moronic for a first impression.

Straightening up, the woman blinked several times before speaking, keeping that smile with her every moment. "Tell me more about Krista, Mrs. Hansen. When we spoke over the phone, you said she's profoundly deaf, but what activities is she capable of?"

Mom beamed at Krista. "Well, she's totally potty-trained. She can color somewhat in the lines. Debbie has been teaching her the alphabet, and she can write the letters of her name.”

From my experience in teaching a summer nursery school a couple of years ago, Krista did better than most three-year-olds. She also knew numbers up to ten. Not out loud, but if I lined up six crayons and a set of number cards one through ten, she’d pick out the six card when I asked her how many crayons.

Mrs. Denahy said nothing more but turned on her heel and motioned for us to follow. “Let me show you our Threes classroom and the outdoor play area.”

We walked down a gray-green hall that smelled of musty books and a strong ammonia floor cleaner. The lady opened the fourth door to our right. Inside were two little tables and six miniature chairs parked around each table. A long, low shelf filled with toys sat along the back wall, and child-sized kitchen appliances were arranged against a side wall.

Krista pulled one of the chairs from the table and sat in it grinning at me. She knew it was just her size, like Goldilocks finding Baby Bear’s chair. I slid both her and the chair back to the table close enough so she could rest her elbows on top. She made motions of eating, scooping something from an imaginary bowl, and moving the imaginary spoon to her mouth.

“Yes. Or you could draw a picture on paper or write your letters.” I kneeled at the table and pretended to write and draw.

Krista nodded her understanding.

While Mom and Mrs. Denahy continued to talk, Krista investigated the play kitchen. She discovered the oven door opened and found little pots and pans inside. She pulled them all out, maybe half a dozen, and placed two on the stovetop. She turned the knobs for the burners, found a spoon in the sink, and stirred pretend food.

I grinned. She played house like any other little kid. Mrs. Denahy should be impressed.

She seemed to be when she came over to Krista. "Very nice. What are you cooking?"

But Krista wasn't looking at her. Mrs. Denahy tapped Krista on the shoulder as a way to correct her mistake. When Krista looked around, the teacher repeated the question.

Krista frowned and looked down, her typical response when she didn't understand.

Mrs. Denahy glanced toward Mom for help. "How do you get her to understand?"

"It often takes more than one try. We do a lot of motions. And we try to get her to read our lips on key words."

The woman tried again. She lifted Krista's chin then pointed to the pan. "What food?" She pantomimed eating.

Krista looked a little scared, but she tried to answer. Nodding yes, she put the spoon to her mouth.

"She can't tell you *what* food," Mom said. "She doesn't say many words, but she watches your lips and makes the same shape with her own sometimes."

Mrs. Denahy frowned as if she were trying to figure out how to deal with Krista and a classroom full of other preschoolers in the room. All she'd have to do would be hand Krista crayons and paper and show her an example of what was wanted. Krista would be happy to obey. But it was Mom's job to talk about that. I was supposed to keep my mouth shut. Which got more and more difficult with each moment.

Krista returned to stirring the food. I tried to demonstrate Krista's abilities.

I waved to get her attention and repeated the question "what food" with my voice and with signs. Pointing to the pan, I asked, "Eggs?" I made the sign for *egg*, then pretended to scramble it.

Krista shook her head.

"Soup?" She could read my lips for that word.

Again, she shook her head but pointed to the pot. She transferred the spoon to the pot, gave it a couple of stirs, then brought it to her mouth and slurped the "soup."

Mrs. Denahy made no comment, even though it was obvious Krista had answered the original question of "What food?" Instead, she tapped Krista's shoulder again and pointed to the pans.

"Let's put these away and I'll show you the play area outside."

Krista couldn't understand such a complicated sentence. She stared at the lady waiting for her to say the same thing in a slightly different way.

Mrs. Denahy put one of the pans from the floor into the oven. She motioned for Krista to do the same. But Krista wasn't done playing yet. She shook her head no. Mrs. Denahy's lips tightened. Was the teacher in a hurry? Couldn't she give a little girl a few more minutes to play in the pretend kitchen? Did the woman wish we would go away?

With Krista watching her, Mom said, "Finish. Put the toys away."

Krista knew "finish." *F* is easy to see on a person's lips. But the tiny kitchen was too tempting. She shook her head *no* at Mom, too. She even brought her fingers together in the sign for "no." Kind of like an exclamation point.

Mom's eyebrows rose in warning; Krista's descended into a frown. *Uh-oh.*

Mom took a deep breath and turned to Mrs. Denahy. "I'm sorry. She usually obeys, but if she doesn't, it's difficult. I'm afraid we've wasted your time."

The teacher's hand fluttered in a helpless gesture. "I can see she's a capable little girl in a lot of ways, but... she has to understand my instructions. And I can't ignore the other children while I try different avenues of communication."

"I understand." Mom bent down and started to pick up the pans.

Krista grunted in anger. Mom grasped one of Krista's hands and placed the pan into it, then forced Krista to put the pan in the oven. Krista screeched and struggled against Mom's superior strength. A second pan went into the oven. Krista flung herself backward and sprawled on the floor, kicking, the braces on her legs now dangerous weapons. I rushed to the stove and put the rest of the pots and pans away. Forget about making Krista do it. Just get her out of here. Mom lifted Krista to her feet. Still out of control, Krista threw herself to the ground again.

Mom handed me the car keys. "Run ahead and open the door."

I waited just long enough to make sure Mom successfully hauled Krista off the floor. With arms and legs flailing all over the place, it took skill.

As I fled the church, I heard Mrs. Denahy saying, "I'm so sorry. I'm so sorry."

Me too.

We drove home with the windows rolled up so the entire town couldn't hear Krista's continued screams. It was a good thing we were only five minutes away, or we'd all have passed out from the heat.

I held my hands over my ears and shouted above Krista's wails. "This is all the teacher's fault. If she had just given Krista a few minutes to play, we would've all left the place happy. I'm glad she's not going to that school."

Mom glanced at me before returning her gaze to the road. In that brief second, I noticed lines on her face that didn't use to be there. Lines angled between her brows. Lines curving from the corners of her mouth toward her chin. My mother looked *old.*

How did that happen? Answers flew through my mind.

Finding out this fourth baby wouldn't be normal.

Krista's open-heart surgery.

Doctors who didn't care.

Krista's eye surgery.

Daddy at war.

His crash.

Krista's temper tantrums.

Raising three other kids besides Krista.

Without their father.

And now we'd met a teacher who didn't care—at least, she didn't care *enough.*

I couldn't do anything to erase the lines from Mom's face, but I could do my best not to add more.

Chapter 33:
Summer Dreams

*When will Da-di come
Home? Mah-mi says, "A laahh dime."
Whatever that means.*

Mom, Grandma, and I sat on the deck with glasses of lemonade sweating in our hands.

"Now, it's not certain yet that Krista will be allowed to attend," Mom cautioned, but the nervous jiggle of her leg informed me she *really* hoped it was certain. "I filled out the application, and Sister Ignatius let me know the cerebral palsy might be a problem."

We had found out about this little school in such a weird way, I knew it had to be God. My dad had talked to the Catholic chaplain on his base in Thailand. The chaplain had served a parish on Long Island. He knew about Commack School for the Deaf, and he knew the school *administrator*. What were the odds?

Dad called Mom. (She nearly had a heart attack getting an overseas phone call from a war zone.) The priest called Sister Ignatius. Mom called the school. The sister agreed to a meeting. And lights, camera, action.

"I wasn't the only pregnant woman with German measles, you know," Mom continued. "In the past, the school has only had room for eight to twelve students per class. They're trying to expand for all these kids born during the epidemic."

Grandma dabbed a handkerchief to her hairline. "Do they have room for fifty or more children?"

My faith in Krista's acceptance faltered. Only eight kids per grade? They must have received over ten times that many applications.

I refused to worry about it. Listening to good news with fresh salty air caressing my face and a tall lemonade in my hand let me think all was right with the world, even if my father was still fighting in Vietnam and my sister had a gazillion problems to solve over her lifetime. Krista would go to school. And they'd teach her how to talk, how to read lips, and how to live in a hearing world.

Mom took a sip of her drink before responding to Grandma's question. "I don't know the numbers. I just know they're adding three classrooms."

She set down the glass and leaned forward clasping her hands together, fingers intertwined. "And get this. She told me she has a meeting scheduled with the governor!

"Apparently, the state has been whining about putting out money for handicapped children like Krista and says the local schools should deal with it themselves. Sister Ignatius knows if the deaf school doesn't have the funds to help all the extra children, the families will have nowhere to go. So, she's determined to change the governor's mind. Her exact words to me were, 'If I have to, I'll march into the man's office and pound on his desk till he understands schools like ours *can* teach your child *if* the state will help us out.'" Mom leaned back into her seat with a triumphant smile.

"She sounds like quite a dynamo," Grandma said.

"I've never met anyone like her." Mom jumped to her feet. "I need to write to Grant right away. If he can keep talking to the priest on the base, and the priest stays in touch with the school, maybe our persistence will be enough to get Krista in."

Grandma's eyes twinkled in agreement. "The squeaky wheel gets the grease."

"It's kind of far, though, isn't it?" I asked.

Mom shrugged off my concern. "A forty-five-minute drive. Oh, another thing. They provide bus service, too, and they drive all over the Island. I won't have to make the trip twice a day."

"So, she has to sit on a bus for forty-five minutes each way?" I *walked* to school, and it only took twenty minutes.

Wait a minute. Driving around Long Island picking up kids must take a lot longer than forty-five minutes.

Mom had already figured it out. "She'll be on the bus for over an hour each way, unfortunately."

"Two *hours* on a bus every, single day?" I'd been terrified that my parents would decide to send Krista to boarding school since the local preschool visit had been a disaster, but this option didn't seem so good anymore either.

Mom regarded me, her lips pursed, her eyes cold.

Didn't she remember what it was like to ride a bus? The uncomfortable seats? The bumpy ride? The bullies? The noise? Although noise wouldn't bother

Krista. On long trips, I passed the time by reading. Poor Krista couldn't even do that.

"Tell me what you'd prefer, Debbie. Do you want your sister to live at a boarding school for the deaf? Do you want her to stay home and learn almost nothing? Or do you want her to go to a school where she can come home every afternoon and she'll learn from teachers who are trained to help deaf children?" Mom savored another sip from her glass and waited for my response.

There was a fourth option. "*I* could teach her."

"No. You couldn't."

Grandma shifted in her seat, a worried frown marred her porcelain features. "Debbie *has* taught Krista the whole alphabet."

Mom glared at her, and Grandma glanced away
Thanks for trying, Grandma.

Mom didn't look quite so ferocious when she turned her attention back to me. "I know you're a good teacher, but you're not a *trained* teacher. And that's what Krista needs right now Not just reading letters and words but saying them."

I slumped against the back of my chair. Yeah, Krista recognized all the letters of the alphabet, but she couldn't say them, couldn't even read my lips half the time. She recognized letters because I finger-spelled them.

The whole inside of me sighed in surrender. *If Krista got accepted to this school, then dealing with a long bus ride was the price to pay for learning to talk.*

This summer before high school had been so much

more fun than last year. Sure, Melissa and Leigh and their group hardly ever spoke to me, but Ronni was a better friend than all of them put together. If it weren't for her, my life would be the pits all the time.

Ronni and I crushed over the boys who came out from The City for the summer. We always stopped on the bridge crossing the bay on our way home from the beach, and we waved to all the cute guys in their little boats—dinghies with motors stuck on the back ends. We ignored the fancy yachts. Those belong to the fathers of the suntanned boys in their dinghies.

Every time Ronni and I hung out on Main Street, we went to the general store where I bought coloring books for Krista--that little kid was going to have plenty to keep her busy on a school bus—and then we gawked at the tourists in their outrageous get-ups or peeked into the posh boutiques and wished we had money. We couldn't even sit at a café and order a soda. Only restaurants in Hollywood or the Hamptons sold sodas for a dollar a glass. The rest of the country spent about twenty cents for the exact same drink.

The stores weren't busy in the middle of the week, so on a Tuesday, Ronni and I worked up our courage and walked inside one of the ritzy little shops to try on fifty-dollar dresses. Just for the fun of it. Wow! Clothes really do make the girl. Our five-dollar outfits from the discount store in Riverhead didn't compare.

We looked gorgeous. Maybe the mirrors in the store made a person look slimmer. On second thought, Ronni looked the same in the mirror as she did standing in front of me, so I really looked that good.

The saleswoman adjusted the spaghetti strap on Ronni's dress. "The white looks exquisite against your tan, but the pink is really cute, too. Which one do you want?"

"Oh, we can't afford either one," Ronni said with a smile. "But they *are* beautiful."

The woman kicked us out of the store. Not with the toe of her strappy sandal, but with her lacquered index fingernail pointing to the door.

We ran down the sidewalk unable to control our giggles.

"Did you see the look on her face?" Ronni mimicked the woman's expression, her lips in a straight line, her nose in the air. "Out. Only *real* shoppers are allowed in here. Out. Out. Out."

"Oh, dahling." I attempted a British accent. "That frock is soooo exquisite on you. White is your color."

"Yeah, what a liar. Anything to sell a dress." She held out her arm to display the lightest of tans. "I look terrible in white. I'll need a pink wedding gown so I don't look like I died."

"The bride *has* to wear white," I said. "Just wear scads of make-up."

Ronni rolled her eyes.

"Really," I insisted. "We'll get you a professional make-up artist like movie stars have. You'll look fabulous. Besides," I added with a sly smile, "I look good in pink, too. Have your bridesmaids wear pink."

"Mmmm." Ronni's face took on a dreamy look as we turned onto Beach Road. "I want my bridesmaids wearing aqua and peach dresses, and we'll have a beach wedding on a Caribbean Island."

A hoot of laughter exploded out of me. "We already have a beach!"

"I want the dresses to *match* the color of the sea.

Not this green-brown water up north."

"And how are we all going to get to a tropical island? Your dad can't pay for everybody."

"I will have a very rich husband." She smirked and raised an eyebrow daring me to disagree.

I played along. "Okay, which do I get to wear, the peach or the aqua? I'm okay with either one."

She stopped on the side of the road to consider. Cocking her head, she stared at me as I posed in the sunshine like a model on a runway.

After strutting forward and back in the middle of the street for a solid minute, I stopped in a final position with one hand on my hip and the other up in the air like one of *The Price Is Right* girls offering a trip around the world. If today were Saturday, a dozen cars would've run over me by now. "How hard can it be? Peach or aqua?"

Totally serious, she nodded. "I think I'll put you in peach. My sister will be maid of honor, and she looks better in the aqua."

"*Vicki* will be your maid of honor? You two fight all the time."

"Yeah, but she's my only sister. It's the right thing to do."

"I guess." I dropped the television model routine and ambled to the grass at the edge of the road. "I only have one sister, but I doubt she'll be my maid of honor unless I'm way past twenty-five when I get married." I sighed. "Which is pretty old.

"Besides, I can't picture a teen-aged Krista. Will she be able to talk with everyone at a wedding reception by then? She can't even say her name yet."

Ronni nudged my elbow. "She can be a junior

bridesmaid. My mom was eighteen when she got married, and her sister was twelve. Aunt Liz got to be the junior bridesmaid since she was too old to be a flower girl."

"Yeah, that might work."

"What colors do you want for *your* wedding? What does Krista look good in?"

I twirled back onto the road, my arms outspread as if I were Maria from *The Sound of Music*. "I want mint green and deep red, almost purple."

"Ooooh!" Ronni squealed. "I look great in both those colors."

The property on the other side of the sidewalk happened to be adorned with a line of rose bushes. Like a rainbow, they ranged from red to pink to peach to yellow. She plucked a deep red bloom and brushed it against her cheek as if to say, "See how beautiful I look in crimson?"

I nodded in appreciation. "And since Krista will probably be a junior bridesmaid, you would still be my maid of honor."

Ronni chose a rose with peach petals and handed it to me with a smile.

I pointed to her flower. "And Krista looks best in dark red. I think they call it burgundy. So, you would wear the pale green."

Arm in arm, we continued down the road to my house. The ocean breeze ruffled our hair, and the sun warmed our faces.

"Wanna put these roses in Paul's tent?" Ronni asked.

"Yeah. He'll hate that." Nothing like a harmless prank to take "the man of the house" down a peg or two.

One more month and the real man of the house would be home. If every day could be like this one, the waiting would be easy.

Chapter 34:
Water Fight

They laughed at first, but
So much water, so much blood.
Wam-ma cried. I cried.

While Mom attended some fancy-schmancy ladies tea, Paul, Wade, and I were each allowed to have one friend over. Her instructions: 1) Boys stay outside. 2) Everyone stay out of Grandma's hair.

Sounded easy. The four boys started some kind of war game in the woods, and Paul's tent was their fort. Ronni and I lounged on the deck, drinking ice-cold vanilla cream sodas and talking about boys and what it'd be like in high school. Krista wandered from the house to the deck to the tent and ambled back inside.

Leave it to a bunch of guys to ramp up the action with a water fight. Their imaginary battles morphed into reality. Paul and Ricky, the twelve-year-olds, against Wade and Larry, the eleven-year-olds. Using the garden hose, they filled up buckets and tossed the water at each other.

"Hey!" I bellowed. "Don't throw the water near the deck. You're getting us wet."

Ricky aimed for the deck and swung the bucket. Water splattered past my knees. He laughed, and Paul laughed with him. Mom would hear about this. Inclining my head toward the house, Ronni followed me inside. We leaned against the washer and dryer and watched the battle intensify from behind the glass storm door.

Wade approached the hose with empty bucket in hand. Paul stood between Wade and the hose. He lifted his full bucket. "I dare you to get closer."

Wade darted around him and raced up the steps to the deck. Paul followed while Ricky blocked Wade's exit down the opposite steps. Wade retreated to the storm door. Paul swooped his bucket forward. A wall of water slammed against the door reminding me of an ocean wave.

Wade stood there, dripping. "You're gonna pay for this!"

Whoa! Where did he learn the words that followed?

I stepped outside. "Paul, you're getting everything wet. Cut it out. Stay on the grass."

"You're not my boss, and you're not my mother." Paul tried to stare me down, but he was the one to look away first, muttering, "If I want to throw water *inside* the house, I'll do it."

He ran back to the hose and filled up the bucket. Staring at me, he poured it slowly on the deck, the look on his face saying, "What are you gonna to do about it?"

I ignored him. Wade, who had refilled his bucket at the sink, opened the door.

I followed him outside. "Wade. Go throw water in his tent. See how he likes *that*."

A wicked grin lit up Wade's face.

Paul blocked his path. "If you throw water in my tent, I'll kill you."

Wade glared at him and started down the steps.

Paul followed, repeating his threat. At the entrance to the tent, Wade hesitated.

I called to him. "Hey, Wade, come here."

He looked my way, and I motioned for him to get back on the deck. Paul smirked and sauntered back to the hose. "Wimp."

I met Wade at the top of the steps and whispered close to his ear. "If you throw the water in the tent, I'll hold the door open so you can run in. Then I'll lock it to keep Paul out, and you lock the front door."

A determined glitter filled Wade's eyes. "Yeah, let's see who's the wimp."

Still holding the full pail, he trotted to Larry, where they huddled together refining the plan.

I grinned at Ronni. "Take Krista to the family room. Wade'll need a clear space once he's through the door. I don't want him tripping over Krista."

Ronni, the perfect teammate, grinned back and grabbed Krista's hand. "This is gonna be good."

She led Krista away. They stopped as soon as they entered the room and peeked around the corner.

I took my position at the door. Wade looked my way. One short jerk of a nod from me and the game was on.

Larry ran full tilt at Paul, sacrificing himself to a

bucketful of water. At the same time, Wade ran to the tent, threw the water—pail and all—into the opening. Without slowing down, he hightailed it for the storm door which I held open.

When Paul saw the bucket sail into his tent, he dropped his pail and raced for the opposite steps in an attempt to intercept Wade. Wade leapt into the house, spun a quick left into the kitchen, and slid along the linoleum floor all the way to the opposite wall, he was that wet. I pulled the door shut and slid the lock just as Paul grabbed the handle. He banged on the glass in fury. He hadn't been this mad since his two-year-old temper tantrums, the same wild anger and howls. His face had turned purple.

"Open the door, Debbie. I'm gonna kill him. Open the door!"

I watched his fist hammer the glass. "Paul! Stop it. You'll break the—"

He punched through the door, and I jumped back with a shriek as glass shards covered the laundry room floor, creating a carpet of diamonds.

Ronni screamed. Krista wailed. Then silence.

Staring at the mess, I knew *big trouble* didn't begin to describe where we were.

"Paul, look what you did. *Look* what you *did!*"

"Will you let me in now?" His voice was strangely quiet.

When I raised my eyes from the floor, I stifled another scream and rushed to unlatch the door. A fountain from Paul's wrist arced into the air. A dark circle of blood had already formed on the deck.

Paul's sneakers crunched on broken glass as he walked calmly to the kitchen sink keeping his thumb pressed against the wound. In the second it took for him to release the pressure and turn on the cold water, the red fountain spurted above the sink. It cast a trail of blood on the counter and a scarlet spatter on the window before he resumed the pressure.

Grandma ran into the room. She stopped so abruptly she had to grab the edge of the kitchen table to keep from pitching forward. "Oh, dear God, what happened?"

Grandma never handled situations with blood. I hoped she wouldn't faint.

She wrung her hands like you read about in books. "What are we going to do? I don't have a number for your mother. She didn't leave a number."

"Check the upstairs phone book." I needed to get her out of the kitchen.

She ran back upstairs, amazingly spry for a seventy-year-old woman. The number was unlisted, but her wasted errand gave me time to think.

The pressure from Paul's thumb continued its job as he held his forearm under the stream of water. At least I didn't have to find out if I could tie a tourniquet.

Mom always kept emergency numbers posted on the wall next to the phone. We'd never needed them. Until now. When I connected with the base clinic, I described Paul's wrist. They dispatched an ambulance.

Krista huddled against me, sobbing into my leg while I stood in the doorway between the kitchen and laundry room. I stroked her hair as the surreal scene came into better focus. Just Paul, Krista, and me. Our friends had disappeared. Wade's distant blubbering could be heard from the back bedroom.

While we waited for the ambulance, I stole glances

at the laundry room floor transformed into a layer of razor-sharp crystals sparkling in the sun. Mostly, I watched Paul. And he watched me, neither of us saying a word. Was he sorry he lost his temper, or did he totally blame me? *I* blamed me. A responsible babysitter? My juvenile, stupid plan resulted in blood and glass and almost killed my brother.

"Paul? I'm sor—"

He cut me off with a terse response. "*You* didn't do this." He lifted his hand from the bleeding wrist, and the ominous red fountain resumed its arc before he quickly clamped pressure back on it.

With the sound of approaching sirens, Grandma returned to the kitchen, still wringing her hands and tearful. No listing in the phone book. The ambulance screeched to a stop in front of our house within five minutes of my call. Scary. The drive to the base normally took ten minutes or more. One corpsman hustled Paul into the ambulance. The other instructed Grandma to send Mom over as soon as we located her.

He stopped to inspect *me*. "Are you okay? Maybe we should take you, too."

Puzzled, I looked down. Streaks of drying blood created striped designs all over my arms and legs. The glass must have hit me on its way to the floor. Nothing hurt. I licked my finger and cleaned off one of the dribbled stains revealing a tiny puncture mark.

"I don't think I need stitches." But maybe I was more hurt than I realized. "Do I?" Maybe I was in shock.

The medic peered closer. "Nah. You just need to clean them up. Soap and water, okay?"

I stared at him. He was leaving me alone with

Grandma and Wade and Krista. And they were all crying. I couldn't handle this.

"Okay," I whispered.

Chapter 35:
Consequences

Where did they take him?
Paw is gone. Da-di is gone.
Who will come home first?

As the ambulance pulled out, lights flashing but no siren, three cars pulled into the driveway, and three couples scrambled out of them. So that's where Ronni, Larry, and Ricky disappeared to. Home. To get help. The dads whistled as they inspected the glass-littered laundry room and the bloodstained deck next to the ruined door. The moms fussed over the rest of us.

Ronni's mom washed down my arms and legs. Crimson stripes were reduced to dozens of red dots. Because, Paul's fist forced everything downward, my face wasn't cut, but glass had rained onto me from my elbows to my feet.

Larry's mom led Wade into the kitchen. He was still blubbering.

"I found him curled up in bed under his covers," she said. "I can't understand a word of what he's saying." She rubbed the back of his neck. "He doesn't seem to be hurt."

His hands covered his face, and he moaned into them. "Deh. Hee..deh. Am…linz…teck...way."

I pulled his hands away. "Wade, it's okay now. Calm down."

He wailed louder. "Deh!"

If he weren't so upset, I would have shaken him "Deh? You mean Dad? You know Dad's not here."

He opened his eyes and glared at me even as his tears dropped to the floor. "Dead! He's dead!"

"Who's dead? Paul?"

"Waaaaaa!"

He covered his face again, but I yanked on his hands. "Paul's not dead. Wade, do you get it? Paul's *not* dead."

He cut off in mid-wail, the stricken look in his eyes replaced by a hint of hope. "But the ambulance took him away."

"They took him to the clinic. He needs stitches."

"He didn't bleed to death?" Wade took a shaky breath and glanced toward the back door. "So much blood."

"He's going to be fine."

His face crumpled once again into tears, and I wrapped him in a hug. He hadn't let me do that since before Krista was born. Over his shoulder, I watched Ricky's mom tending to Grandma. They sat at the kitchen table side by side. Mrs. Callahan had one arm around Grandma's shoulders, and she spoke so quietly I couldn't make out the words. Grandma's shrill sing-song of "I don't know what to do" quieted into low moans.

Larry's mom brought Wade a glass of juice, which he took to the dining room. From that window he could see the dads at work in the back yard.

Krista's fist had never let go of my shorts while Ronni's mom had cleaned me up.

"Are you okay?" I asked. I signed O and K.

"She signed YES then added, "P. O-K?" And she pointed to her wrist. P was our sign for Paul.

I signed YES.

"Big ow," I said.

She raised her arms for me to pick her up. Since she was getting too heavy to hold for long, I set her on the washer, and we watched the dads clean up the mess. One swept up glass while the other two scrubbed at the boards of the deck until most of the bloodstains were gone. As they put away brooms and buckets, Mom walked into the kitchen.

"What's going on? Why are there so many cars--" Her gaze widened, the whites of her eyes glistening all around her irises. She pressed her purse and keys against her chest so hard I could see one key making a dent in the skin near her collarbone.

She heard "Paul," "ambulance" and "clinic," and she backed out of the kitchen, thanking the people who came to help before running to the car and speeding down the road.

The three families went back to their homes once clean-up was complete. Someone had even taken down the tent and hung it over the deck railing to dry. Ronni's mom returned momentarily with a pizza from the restaurant on the highway. Usually, pepperoni and mushroom was our favorite, but nobody enjoyed it. Wade and I took careful bites, not leaving a sliver of melted cheese, like it was the last meal before our execution.

I had failed. As a babysitter. As a sister. As a daughter. I had promised Daddy I would help Mom, and what had I done? Nearly killed my own brother. Excuses couldn't cut it. I should've prevented the water fight, not chosen a side and joined in the battle.

Mom and Paul arrived home around seven. Krista hurled herself into Mom's arms and started to cry. Other than "P. O-K," I hadn't tried to explain to her what happened since Paul left. She probably thought a "big ow" meant Paul had to stay in a hospital like she did when she had a big ow.

Mom jiggled her to calm her down, then held Krista's face so they had eye contact. "Everything's fine, now." She smiled. "Are you fine?"

Krista could see the word *fine* on a person's lips. It worked better for her than trying to see the word *good*. She nodded back at Mom, then buried her face in Mom's neck.

Paul noticed the pizza box on the kitchen table. "We ate pizza, too." He grinned, acting pretty chipper for someone who could've died today. He showed off the heavy bandage around his wrist. "I didn't even take the pain pill they wanted to give me."

Yeah, like he was Superman or something. He may not have needed help with the pain, but I knew the real reason he turned down the pills. He still couldn't swallow them. Mom always mashed them up in a teaspoon of water whenever he needed medicine. Big baby.

Mom held Krista's face again. "Time for sleep. Grandma will put you in pajamas. I will come up and kiss you goodnight, but first, I will talk to these three."

The whole time she talked, she used her hands to act out some of the words. She knew Krista wouldn't be able to read her lips and understand everything. Krista pretty much got the words *sleep*—hand under the cheek, *Grandma*—point to Grandma, *pajamas*—a tug on her clothes. Plus, pajama was easy to see on the lips. Then Mom pointed upward for *upstairs,* kissed Krista's cheek, and pointed to Paul, Wade, and me.

And Mom didn't look too happy.

I swallowed, sick with dread.

Krista made no protest as Mom handed her off to Grandma. Wade and I were still at the table, and Mom guided Paul to an empty chair. He didn't look so sure of himself anymore.

"I want to hear your side of the story," she said to Wade and me. "Paul has already told me his version."

I took a deep breath, and Wade burst into tears.

"It was my fault. I threw water in his tent." He lay his head on his arms and bawled.

Mom patted his head absently and looked at me.

I couldn't hold her gaze. My voice was low. "It was my idea to throw water in the tent."

"What, Debbie? I can't hear you over your brother. Settle down, Wade."

He subsided into some kind of mewling puppy whine.

I lifted my chin, and still without looking at her I spoke louder. "It was my idea to throw water in the tent. And it was my idea to lock the door so Paul couldn't get in."

"So, all of you are equally to blame." Mom sank back in her chair and shook her head. She probably wished Daddy were here to deal with us.

We already knew the verdict. We waited for Mom to pronounce sentence.

Mom lifted Paul's arm so our eyes were directed to the bandages. "Paul and I have discussed the consequences of what happens when a person loses control of his temper. You can see one of those consequences right here. And what if Debbie *hadn't* locked the door? What might Paul have done if he had caught up with Wade? Maybe it would be Wade in the hospital."

The last flicker of Paul's macho man attitude blinked out.

Mom grasped Wade's chin between her thumb and forefinger. "And *you* have made yourself sick with guilt over this. Look how badly you felt thinking Paul had died."

Wade's tears continued to spill down his cheeks.

"And you." She turned to me, disappointment in her eyes. "Sometimes I forget you're not as wise as you appear to be."

After a moment of silence, she sighed. "I'll be assigning you more chores to help pay for replacing the glass in the door."

"You mean I'm not grounded?" I asked.

"You're not gonna spank us?" Wade quavered.

"What chores?" That was Paul.

The corner of Mom's mouth quirked at our chorus. "You're not grounded. Nobody's getting spanked, And I'll make a list of chores." She pushed her chair away from the table. "Oh, and you will write notes of apology to all the parents who came over and helped. Three notes from each of you."

Wade hung his head, but Paul looked at me with an expression of pain on his face. He mouthed the words, "Three?" Maybe I'd let him copy off of mine.

Mom stood and kissed the tops of our heads. "What I can't believe is how you got everything under control before I got home. I have to admit I'm proud of you. You knew first aid. You knew to call for an ambulance. Your friends knew to get help. I'm impressed."

Huh. One of the worst things I'd ever done, and my mother ended up complimenting me.

Chapter 36:
Homecoming

Just Mah-mi and me.
We play every day and we
Drive to the airport.

Time for summer camp. Again. I had never been a happy camper, and some years were worse than others. At least, with the move to California and back we didn't have to go last summer.

Daddy was due home on August seventeenth, four days after this new camp ended. I hoped the week away would speed up the waiting time until he arrived.

If only Ronni could've come with me, but her dad said he already paid for the beach club. He said he wouldn't spend any more money. To make life even worse, my skin had broken out into a dozen pimples. I sure wouldn't dazzle anyone with my beauty.

On Day Two, as I sat on my lower bunk and combed tangles out of my hair, Lisa, whose bunk was across from mine, leaned close to her friend Karen. "Jim told me to meet him behind his cabin after dinner." Lisa giggled. "I can't believe it! This is going to be the best week ever."

Karen hugged her. "The cutest guy in camp. You are so lucky. What are you going to wear?"

Lisa, a skinny brunette who had worn four different halter tops since we arrived, dug deep into her giant suitcase. "I've got something really cute and sparkly in here." With a flourish of victory she held up the scrap of yet another halter top—black and silver this time--and waved it like the starting flag at the Indianapolis 500.

Karen squealed at the gorgeousness of it.

Oh, brother.

As we all got ready for lights out, Lisa hadn't returned to the cabin. I caught snatches of several conversations.

"I wish my boyfriend could've come to camp with me."

"The guy next to me ate four desserts. No wonder he's the size of a whale!"

"I'll gain five pounds if I even eat one dessert."

"My little brother wanted to come here with me. He said he would 'protect me.' He's three."

Gales of laughter followed that last comment. It would never be cool to mention your mother, but it was okay to talk about your kid brother—or sister. There was my opening.

"My little sister is almost three, too. She's deaf. And she had open-heart surgery when she was a baby."

"Wasn't that dangerous?" Karen asked.

"Yeah, it was. But she made it through. Then we found out she has cerebral palsy, so she has to wear leg braces."

Frowns of confusion all around.

"Can she walk?"

"How does she know what you're saying?"

I opened my mouth to answer, and Lisa pranced into the cabin. The girls crowded around her, magpies all atwitter.

"Where have you been?"

"Is Jim as cool as he looks?"

"Did he kiss you?"

Who cares?

My week continued to crawl. Reading books at home would have made the time pass faster. Instead, endless baseball games. I was lucky to get the bat on the ball and forget snagging a pop fly. I was too shy to barge into the ready-made cliques formed last summer. Saturday afternoon couldn't come soon enough. I counted the minutes from activity to activity. Even the hour swimming in the bay felt like an entire afternoon.

Free time was the most excruciating. As we showered off the sand and changed for dinner, girls hung out in little groups. I guess I could've joined one, but no one seemed interested in getting to know me— nobody had ever asked about my sister after Lisa's glorious entrance that night—so why should I be all that interested in their lives either?

On the final evening while the camp staff prepared the dining hall for The Dance, college-age counselors set up some stupid games for an hour after dinner. The worst one was where you hold an orange under your chin and pass it on to the next person in line, who must also hold it under their chin, all without using hands. If the orange drops, you can pick it up, put it under your chin, and try again.

Of course, each team lined up boy, girl, boy, girl. Nothing like encouraging hot romance between teen campers. The guy who passed the orange to me had more acne than I did. I tried to avoid the point of my chin on his pink-puffed neck. Which meant I dropped the orange.

"Sorry," I said.

"It's okay." He placed it back under his chin.

I either had to touch that neck or drop it again. *Sacrifice for the team, Debbie.* He grinned at me after the successful exchange. His friendly smile surprised me out of my Attitude. Peter. That's right. His name was Peter.

Then it was time to pass the orange on to the guy on my other side, who was drop-dead gorgeous. The famous Jim. No pimple dared to erupt on that perfectly bronzed skin.

Apparently, the one blemish left on my chin was one too many for him. We dropped the orange three times.

"Just hold still," he told me with a frown. On his other side, Lisa glared at me like I was trying to steal her boyfriend.

Feeling like a chastened kindergartener, I obeyed. He rolled it to the side of my neck and grabbed it from there.

The games ended. My team lost. The dance began.

Jim and Lisa were first on the floor as some disc jockey blasted "Happy Together." Other couples of the week joined them. I stood next to three girls from my cabin who hadn't gotten lucky in the "true love" department either.

After several songs, Peter sauntered by. "You wanna dance?"

The DJ set the needle on another fast tune.

"Okay." I stepped out on the floor with him. Why not? I liked to dance. I'd seen other girls turning him down. Would they rather be bored the whole night?

We stuck with each other for the whole two hours. Neither of us said much of anything, although on slow dances I received a lot of "sorries." He kept stepping on my feet.

Which made me think of how I used to dance *on* my dad's feet when I was little. We'd eat dinner at the officers' club, and afterwards a live band would play. Daddy would dance with me, and then he'd take a turn with Mom. Those were the best times.

Another crushing pain to my toe jolted me out of memories.

"Sorry," Peter said.

The next morning, campers packed up, swept the cabin, and "enjoyed" a final Bible study, like anyone's mind was on God. Either we were desperate to go home, or we were crying into our King James Versions because the camp romance was finished. Promises to write and be faithful forever would be broken in a week, and everyone knew it.

I endured a final baseball tourney with a break for lunch. Parents were due to arrive around two. Kids hung out with their soon-to-be-ex-buddies. When somebody's mom arrived, the kid gave her a nonchalant wave, hugged her friend, then ambled off to get her gear. The prime directive to the end: Never Let Your Parents See You Care.

I figured I could play that game, too. I stood at the fringe of one group acting like I belonged there. Once Mom arrived, I would make some kind of "nice knowing you" comment, get my stuff out of the cabin, and head toward the station wagon. *Then* I'd squeeze the stuffings out of Krista. And Mom.

What had Krista done all week as an only child? Gotten lots of Grandma attention. Grandma was great for going on walks or playing Go Fish.

Our big blue wagon pulled into the parking lot. I'd wait until Mom stepped out of the car before running through my play-it-cool script with the girl standing closest to me.

But Mom didn't emerge from the driver's side door.

I gasped. "Ohh."

The girl on my right looked at me like I might throw up on her sandals. "You okay?"

Yes!

My feet flew across the ground, and I slammed into Daddy for the hug of a lifetime.

I didn't care if the other kids laughed at the girl crying in her father's arms. I didn't care if they thought I was the dorkiest kid at camp. A baby. When it came right down to it, I *was* my dad's baby. And I always would be.

Before I could say a word, someone tugged on my shorts.

Krista.

She pointed to Daddy, and with a grin as wide as the Atlantic Ocean, she opened her fist to reveal our two pebbles. Their green stripes glinted in the sunlight.

Book Discussion Questions

1. Debbie and Francie had managed to hold onto their friendship for two years after Debbie had moved away. Have you ever had to leave a friend or did you have a friend who moved away from your town?

2. If you answered *yes*, were you able to keep the friendship going for a long time even though you lived far away from each other?

If *yes,* how did you make the friendship work?

If *no*, what do you think happened that you are no longer friends?

3. In chapters three and four, what words does the author use that show how Debbie, her brothers and her mom felt about moving day?

4. What differences did Debbie notice between New York and California as the family traveled to their new house in the desert?

5. In the California house, Debbie and Krista didn't share a bedroom. Do you think Debbie and her parents did the right thing by forcing Krista to sleep in her own room? Why or why not?

6. Debbie had never met up with prejudice against Hispanics before. What was your opinion of the group of girls she had to deal with on her first day at the school in California? Did Debbie do the right thing? How would you have handled that situation?

7. Debbie was surprised when Nora Jean befriended her. What is your opinion of Nora Jean? What were her good qualities? What were her not-so-good qualities?

8. In Book One, *Reaching Into Silence*, doctors had said Krista would never be able to learn. What kinds of things do you see Krista learning throughout *Dancing in the Silence?*

9. When Debbie left California, she and Nora Jean exchanged gifts. (HINT: keep those in mind for Book Three, *Speaking Through the Silence!)* Do you think their gifts to one another were good choices? Why or why not?

10. What did Debbie and her brothers promise their dad they would do while he was gone to war?

11. How did they keep their promise? How did they break it?

12. Grandma is introduced in this book of the World Without Sound series. How would you describe her?

13. When Debbie tried to meet up with her old friends before school started, what was her horrible surprise? Were *you* surprised that this happened to her?

14. How did Ronni make Debbie's first day of school so much better than she expected?

15. Sometimes, Paul and Wade drove Debbie crazy. Other times, she was so glad they were her brothers. Name one way they made her angry. Name

one way they showed her how much they loved her.

16. How did you feel when you first read that Debbie's dad was in a jet crash?

17. At first, Debbie was terrified of Artie. Why did her feelings change?

18. Do you think it was a good idea for the kids to keep "Life Stones" until their father returned? Why or why not?

19. Was Debbie right to feel angry with the teacher at the one nursery school they visited? Why or why not?

20. If one of your parents had been gone for a long time and then they surprised you by arriving at school, how do you think you would react?

Enjoy the first chapter of *Speaking Through the Silence,* Book Three of the World Without Sound series.

Chapter 1: Temper Tantrums (August 1968)
Six, nine? Or nine, six?
I don't know. They look the same!
They make me so mad!

***

My little sister displayed four cards for her latest collection in Go Fish. Three nines and a six. Krista was good at recognizing numbers, but since she wasn't quite three years old, nines and sixes looked pretty much the same.

I shook my head and pointed to the mismatched card. Krista's proud smile disappeared. I spread out the cards so she could see them clearly, but she wouldn't look at them. Instead, she stared daggers at me.

After gathering the four cards, I returned them to her. She fired them at my face.

"Stop it." I signed the word for *stop* and offered the cards to her again. "Do you want to play, or not?"

Krista accepted the cards with hooded eyelids and a tightening of her lips. Mad, but not out of control. She locked her gaze on mine and with perfect control, threw the cards at me a second time.

Here we go again. All I'd wanted was to do something fun with her while we waited for dinner. Without breaking eye contact, I shook my finger at her. BAD. I signed the word and flung my hand straight toward her. YOU-BAD.

"Yeeeeeeee!" Her voice rose like a tea kettle on full steam. She picked up the rest of the deck and threw it at me.

Being deaf didn't give her an excuse to be a brat. I grabbed several of the cards and threw them back at her. I was entering my freshman year in high school and she had me behaving like a kindergartner.

When Krista lunged for me, I grabbed her around the waist with one arm and lugged her to the back door. No easy feat. She might be skinny, but with the metal ankle-to-thigh braces sheathing her legs, lifting her felt like carrying a loaded garbage can to the curb. My free hand turned the handle, and I hoped those lethal legs didn't kick through the new storm door. They shouldn't. After my thirteen-year-old brother Paul punched through the glass last month (long story—he deserved to be locked out), Mom replaced it with acrylic. Nobody wanted more blood splattered all over the house. *Or* another ambulance run.

My parents and grandmother waited for an explanation on the deck as I dumped Krista beside Daddy lounging in one of our newest lawn chairs. If anyone could get her to behave, he could.

"We were playing Go Fish, and all of a sudden, she's throwing the cards everywhere and screaming at me because I told her a nine and a six are *not* the same number. Which she already knows."

I slumped on the picnic bench, finding no pleasure in the ocean breeze, while Krista continued to jabber and screech at me. She was really hard to deal with sometimes. She couldn't see our words, and doctors told us we weren't supposed to use sign language, so how could we get any kind of message across? I had learned *some* sign language—the doctors could go fly a kite—but I didn't study it like I studied Spanish. Which meant I didn't know enough to help Krista all the time.

Even when I signed, like with the card game, she still lost her temper. Terrible Twos reigned supreme.

With Krista still shrieking at me—no words—just high-pitched, angry squeals, Daddy grasped her shoulders and turned her around to face him. He raised his eyebrows and gazed directly into her eyes. She dissolved into tears and hid her face in his lap.

She and I were totally alike when it came to Daddy. We couldn't stand to disappoint him. And it wasn't just the fact that he'd only been home for two weeks after a year spent fighting in Vietnam. I still hadn't stopped saying in my head, "Thank you, God," every time he pulled into the driveway.

Daddy rubbed Krista's back in soothing circles, something that used to calm me down, too. "Go get the cards that started the trouble," he told me.

I made sure the adults heard my martyred sigh as I pushed off from the bench. With fifty-two cards scattered all over the den, I searched every corner to find the four I needed. When I returned, Krista was cuddled into Daddy's chest. She threw a sullen look my way, then shifted her position so her back was turned to me.

I held out the cards. "Nine of hearts, nine of spades, nine of clubs, six of diamonds. She thinks they all match. At least, that's what I think she thinks."

Daddy grouped them so their corners were right next to each other. Obviously, three numbers had a circle at the top and the fourth a circle at the bottom. He tapped Krista. She looked up, noticed the cards, and burrowed her face against Daddy.

He flipped Krista so she was forced to sit with her back against him, then held the cards in front of her. He pointed to the corners.

She whimpered.

"Honey, if she starts in again, can we leave this for another time?" Mom was sick of tantrums, too.

Grandma stepped inside with her magazine and iced tea. She hated loud noises.

Daddy handed the cards back to me. "Hold two in each hand."

I muttered under my breath. "This isn't gonna be pretty."

"Debbie." His voice held warning.

I thrust the cards close to Krista's face.

Daddy pushed them a few inches away and leaned forward so Krista could see his lips. He pointed to each nine. "What number?"

With a pout, Krista held up five fingers on one hand and four on the other.

Daddy nodded and pointed to the six. "What number?"

The pout tightened to a grim line. She held up five fingers on one hand and *four* fingers on the other.

"A nine?" His eyes opened wide in surprise. He swiveled his head in an exaggerated motion as if he were examining all the cards carefully. "Nine. Nine. Nine." Pause. "And nine?"

What a ham. Krista stared at him, not impressed with his antics.

"Debbie, put the nines in one hand and the six in the other, then bring the cards closer to my face."

I stood to one side keeping the cards a couple of

inches from Daddy's nose. He leaned even closer so one eyeball was almost on a number nine. He looked at Krista. "Nine?"

She nodded. The pout was gone from her eyes. Her lips remained tight, but the corners began to curve up.

Daddy leaned so close to the number six card that his face touched it. He pulled back and looked at Krista, his eyes wider than ever. "Nine?"

He returned to peering at the six. A little snort escaped from Krista. Daddy's head snapped to face her again, and a startled giggle erupted.

"Nine?"

She started to nod, but he raised his eyebrows in a "think again" expression. Krista leaned closer to the six card. Circle on the lower portion of the number. She glanced at Daddy, back to the number. She darted a look at me, then back to the six, then back to Daddy.

"Nine?" he repeated.

Krista hung her head. Slowly, she lifted five fingers of one hand and the thumb of the other. And I had called my baby sister "bad." *What was my problem?*

When she raised her head, she found me kneeling beside the chair, my arms opened wide. She slid off of Daddy's lap for a hug. The only way she knew to say, "I'm sorry."

Mom stood and picked up her glass, plus Daddy's. "This is why we need to find a school. She's got to learn to communicate without all the tears. It's exhausting for all of us, and it's not fair to her." She headed for the door. "Dinner will be ready in ten minutes."

Linda Sammaritan writes realistic fiction, mostly for kids ages ten to fourteen. She has completed a middle grade trilogy, **World Without Sound**, based on her own experiences growing up with a deaf sister. Book One, *Reaching Into Silence*, was an ACFW Genesis Contest semi-finalist and a First Impressions Finalist.

Linda had always figured she'd teach teens and tweens until school authorities presented her with a retirement wheelchair and rolled her out the door. However, God changed those plans when He gave her a growing passion for writing fiction. In May of 2016, she blew goodbye kisses to her students and dedicated her work hours to becoming an author.

A wife, mother of three, and grandmother to eight, Linda regales the youngest grandchildren with "Nona Stories," tales of her childhood. Maybe one day those stories will be in picture books!

Where Linda can be found on the web:

www.lindasammaritan.com

www.facebook.com/lindasammaritan

www.twitter.com/LindaSammaritan

www.instagram.com/lindasammaritan

www.ingramcontent.com/pod-product-compliance
Lightning Source LLC
Chambersburg PA
CBHW070443200726
48293CB00007B/2110